NED KELLY
&
The City of the Bees

NED KELLY & the City of the Bees

THOMAS KENEALLY

illustrated by Stephen Ryan

DAVID R. GODINE PUBLISHER

Boston

First U.S. hardcover edition published in 1981 *by*
David R. Godine, Publisher, Inc.
Box 9103
Lincoln, Massachusetts 01773

First softcover edition published 1995.

Library of Congress Cataloging in Publication Data

Keneally, Thomas
Ned Kelly and the city of the bees
p. cm.

SUMMARY: During a bout of appendicitis Ned Kelly is reduced to the size of a bee and spends the summer in a beehive.
[1. Bees -- Fiction. 2. Beehives--Fiction. 3. Australia--Fiction.]
I. Ryan, Stephen. ill. II. Title.
III. Title: Ned Kelly and the city of the bees.
PZ7.K36NE 1984 [Fic]--dc20
ISBN 1-56792-022-5

Printed in the United States of America

To Jane and Margaret,
my daughters, who talked me into writing this story

Note for the American Edition

THE STORY OF how Ned Kelly spent a summer in a bee hive, in the company of a 120-year-old girl called Nancy Clancy and the bees of Selma's kingdom, is set in a country, my country, called Australia. In Australia when I was young I went to a school where the summer uniform was like Ned's—shorts, an athletic vest, sandals, a big hat. I lived in a town like the one where Ned's family lives; I too had a strange experience in the town's hospital.

Perhaps the most important amusement of people in that town when I was a child were radio programs of the kind to which Apis, the worker bee, listens in this book. Some of these programs were romantic, others were adventurous, and people—like Apis—went to a lot of trouble to make sure they heard the next episode of their favorite serial. My favorite was called *The Search for the Golden Boomerang*, and, although I can hardly remember the story line, I mention it in the book because of the joy it gave me then.

Australia is different from America in many ways. Notably, the seasons are the reverse of American seasons. You will see that in the story: August is winter, December is summer. But you will notice, later in the book, a likeness between America and the Australia of my childhood and Ned's. The stealing of cattle was common—ordinary men took cattle, often because times were hard and money was scarce. Americans call the crime 'rustling,' Australians—as you'll see—call it 'duffing.'

You will also notice that just as there were Indians in the forest and on the great plains of America before the whites came, there were in Ned's valley and mine a race we call the aborigines of Australia. It was these sensitive people who comforted Nancy Clancy when she was lost in the Australian wilderness.

I hope you enjoy this story. I have lived in Connecticut and have known American children, and it gives me great pleasure to think that they might take this book in their hands and, best of all, enjoy it.

TOM KENEALLY

Contents

1

Ned Kelly in Hospital

WHEN I WAS a small boy, I spent a whole summer with wild honey bees in their nest in the hollow of an old mountain ash. Before you start laughing at the idea, you'd better listen to what I have to say.

I lived in a warm valley then. A broad, snaky river ran through the valley and many blossoms grew on its banks. Bees were always visiting the blossoms collecting sugary nectar from them, rolling their fat little bodies against the pollen—that dust, often yellow, sometimes even purple, you can see in the insides of flowers and pick up with your fingers. Although it is not always kind to people, that dust, making some sneeze and others wheeze, the bees feed their infants on it.

I knew that some of the bees belonged to farmers and lived in neat white hives that the farmers made for them. Farmers' bees would take the dusty pollen and the sweet nectar they had collected back to the owners' hives. They would use up the pollen and make honey from the nectar. Only some of this honey would they use themselves, and then the farmer would collect the extra honey out of the white hive and sell it to the people. The bees didn't mind, although in the streets of our town you sometimes saw unlucky farmers with swollen faces or hands from bee stings. But farmers have been building hives for bees and taking honey from them for thousands of years. For honey is, as everyone knows, good for humankind.

But there are other bees. They are the wild honey bees. They make honey only for themselves and for their ruler, the queen of their wild hive. Sometimes I saw their hives in holes in the trunks of trees. Or in the walls of some derelict farmhouse where some poor family had gone broke and had to leave home. The wild bees knew how to find a place that was shady and away from the wind, a place that would not fill up with water when it rained, a place that was high enough to be beyond the reach of most ground-level nuisances—rats or mice or opossums.

At the time of my meeting with the bees I was of course a schoolchild in our warm valley. In fact, so warm was it in our valley in summer-time that our school uniform was: a straw hat, a vest, and a pair of brown shorts. You can get some idea of how I looked then from the drawing.

The girls wore light frocks. For example, my friend Jack Horne had a sister called Kate. They were so poor that Kate's frock was made of flour bags. Those two were my best friends, and we used to walk to school together and walk back again. I remember that sometimes the tar on the roads would be so hot we'd have to hop across like kangaroos. It was two miles to school, two miles home, but there was always something fresh to see—a funeral, or a circus setting up at the showground, or a Chinese vegetable seller, or a long goods train held up at the station, or one of the Indian traders coming to town with his camels.

On the day I first met the bees, I began feeling dizzy as soon as I left the school gate. There was a terrible pain in my leg. My body felt heavier than the earth. Jack and Kate Horne ran through the town but I dragged behind them.

At last I sat down on a grass footpath. The right side of my stomach felt large with pain. I looked at the hill leading up to my house and knew I could not climb it. Jack and Kate Horne ran back to me.

"What's the matter?" they said. Then they said, "You look white."

"Hey," I said. "Get my mother, will you?"

"Run and get his mother, Jack," Kate ordered. "Go on."

"Why me?"

"Men are runners," Kate said, "and women are nurses."

Because in those days there weren't many male nurses, or many female runners.

So it was Jack who ran for my mother. Kate went down to a rain-water puddle in the gutter. She dipped a handkerchief in it and wiped my forehead. "Well," she said, "never fear, Nurse Kate is here."

But Nurse Kate did not improve the pain. I lay on my back with my knees up. Kate pushed a twig into my mouth. "Let me take your temperature," she said. I was weak and full of fear and I couldn't stop her doing that sort of thing.

At last I saw my father's old truck come down over the hill. My

father was driving, my mother sat beside him and Jack stood in the back, looking serious. They pulled up by the footpath and my mother jumped out and looked at me. The first thing she did was pull the twig out of my mouth.

"What's a twig doing in your mouth?" she said.

"What's the matter? What's the matter, Ned, mate?" asked my father.

"Aagh!" I said. "My side hurts." And I began to cry. My father got my mother to sit in the front seat. He lifted me into the truck and laid my head on her lap. While he drove as fast as the old truck would go up the hill towards the town hospital, Jack and Kate rode in the back, cheering a lot, as if we were a stagecoach that was outrunning Indians. I thought, I wonder do they care about *me?*

A fussy Sister met us at the hospital door. She looked over her spectacles at my mother and at me in my mother's arms. She looked at my father in his work clothes. Since he worked in a sawmill he was very dusty. Then she looked at Jack and Kate.

"We can't have those grubby children in here," she told us.

My father nodded towards me. "Here's one grubby child you'll have to have."

"Those two can wait outside," she said, pointing in her turn at Kate and Jack. So Kate and Jack stayed at the door, making faces when the Sister's back was turned.

The Sister showed my mother and father a bench where they could lay me. Then she ran to fetch the town's new young doctor, Doctor Morgan. When Doctor Morgan came in he touched my stomach. I squealed with pain.

"That's it," he said. "I'm sure it's appendicitis."

"How do you spell that?" asked Kate. She had crept in behind us because Doctor Morgan was young and friendly and she wasn't as scared of him as of the Sister. Also, she thought she was the best speller in the school and often asked grown-ups to spell things for her.

Doctor Morgan smiled. "APPENDICITIS," he said. "The appendix is a small tube of muscle in the intestine. Sometimes it gets so swollen we have to take it out. Put this boy in a bed, Sister."

As the Sister carried me out, I could hear Kate spelling, showing off. "APPERCIDITMUS."

"Wrong," said Doctor Morgan. "Out!"

At the door, the Sister turned so that I could wave to my mother and father, and to Kate and Jack as they left. I had a feeling that frightened me, that I wouldn't see my parents or Kate or Jack for a long time.

The Sister took me into a hospital ward and put me in a bed that was screened off from all the other beds. There were other children in the ward making a lot of noise. Two boys were having a race on crutches. I saw through a crack in one of the screen curtains a fat boy fall off his crutches.

The Sister called out, "You brats stop that! We have a sick boy here."

Doctor Morgan came to my bed carrying a large syringe.

"This will make you sleepy," he told me. "Then we can operate. You won't feel it much." Doctors have always said that to children since the start of time. Sometimes they are right. But I wasn't worried by the idea of pain. I was lonely. That's what worried me.

The Sister pulled down my school pants, roughly, so that my backside was bare. I didn't like having this done by someone like her. Before I could think of it, the doctor slid the needle in.

2

A Bee and Nancy Clancy

As soon as the medicine went into my body through the point of that needle, I began to feel lighter, sleepier, even a little happier. But when Doctor Morgan left, and the Sister went out too, having dragged my shorts up again, I felt I was the loneliest boy in the world. There were all at once tears all over my cheeks. Yet I was so tired I slept in a second.

When I opened my eyes, I looked at the window sill above my bed. It seemed there were two small creatures up there. One was definitely a bee. I could see the dark and the gold of its little body. The other looked like a small butterfly. They sat there staring at me. I knew by the way they sat that they were interested in everything that had gone on in the hospital ward, that they were watching me the way I watched circuses or strangers arriving in the town. The butterfly didn't flutter, there wasn't a buzz from the bee.

It was normal to see bees on window sills in our town. Funnily, I'd never looked at one before as closely as this. What's a bee's face like? I wondered. Let's see.

The first thing I saw were the eyes. Deep brown. Glossy. I saw something there that I'd never seen in a bee before. Pity. The bee was sorry for me. You know, the way a dog looks at you with eyes full of sorrow. In fact the bee was just like a dog to me. It was handsome. It was furry. I felt I wanted to reach out and pat it. I said, "G'day, feller," the way you do to a dog. At least, the way we used to say to dogs. We used to call the males feller and the bitches girl. It would be a little while before I found out this bee was a female.

As soon as I spoke, the bee whirred its wings and jumped and landed on my chest. It climbed up my vest, coming towards me. Any other time, I would have been frightened of being stung. Bee stings are a nuisance. There's a swelling, and a little black sting stuck in your skin. Some people don't take well to bee stings. Mrs Delahunty who lived on the hill swelled up like a balloon one day when a bee stung her. They'd had to rush her to the hospital. When I was stung, my mother used always to put washing-blue on the place. I wonder what mothers use these days, now that you don't see washing-blue any more.

Of course bee stings are a problem for the bee too. The skin and muscles of humans are like iron to a bee and so, once it stings a human, the bee cannot pull its sting back out. It has to leave the sting there; it has to rip its belly open to get away from the human, and so it dies.

I could tell this bee didn't want to sting me or to die. Its mouth was open like a pup's and a sort of snout hung out like a pup's tongue. And on the end of the snout hung one drop of something golden and glistening.

"Honey for me, feller?" I asked it. But it wasn't honey, not heavy or sticky like honey.

The bee came right up to my chin and dumped the drop of glowing liquid on my bottom lip. Then it walked up my face and sat down near my ear. I licked the golden drop and my body seemed to sigh. I felt warm and golden myself, just as if I was a fresh baked loaf of bread in the window of Bennet's bakery. I closed my eyes a second.

When I opened them the bedclothes and the bed seemed to race away from me in all directions. The bars at the end of the bed seemed far away and high as mountains, growing higher all the time. There I was, lost in a plain of white. I thought that I was dreaming of snow. But it didn't snow in that town, in fact I had never seen snow in my life.

The bee rolled over at my side, the way a large too-playful dog would. At the same time a voice above my head said,

"Play with a bee, my boy, say I
But watch out for the sneezing and the weepy eye."

It was a girl's voice and I looked up. High above us, on the sill, sat a small girl in a blue gingham dress. Earlier, I'd thought she was a butterfly, but she was definitely a girl, her hair done up in old-fashioned corkscrew curls.

No sooner had she warned me about the sneezing and the weepy eyes than I began sneezing and my eyes began to weep.

"You'll get used to that," said someone. It was a husky female voice. I looked at the bee, who had stopped rolling.

"What did you say?" I asked it.

"You'll get used to it," it said. "You got used to it, didn't you, Miss Clancy?"

The little girl sitting on the sill high above us said,

"I got used to it, barely a sneeze
Barely an itch or a scratch or a wheeze."

The bee's husky voice announced, "She's doing everything in rhyme. It's a stage she's going through."

The girl above us yelled.

"I can't help it, it's my fancy,
You see, my name is Nancy Clancy."

The bee explained with a sigh. "That's right. Her name is Miss Nancy Clancy. I wish it wasn't. Maybe if it was Susan O'Leary or something like that, she wouldn't make rhymes all the time."

"And down there," the girl called, "rolling round like an over fed pup, is my friend Apis. You may have noticed she's a bee."

"A worker and a gatherer," said Apis with pride.

"You listen to the radio half the day," Nancy Clancy said.

"Even a worker bee needs her relaxation," said Apis. "Why, there are some bees that gather all day long. They're dead by the end of summer. Worry. Overwork. It's not going to happen to me. I'm going to last the winter, and see another summer come."

"Do you really listen to the radio?"

"At Mrs Abey's place. I like the serials. I like *When a Girl Marries* and *The Search for the Golden Boomerang.* Mrs Abey has a shady sill. I can sit up there quite safe and hear the whole program. How else do you think I learnt to speak so well?"

"Can *you* speak bee?" I asked the girl in the blue gingham dress.

She gave a pitying laugh as if I were a very backward boy.

"In a hive you don't have to speak so well.
It isn't how you talk, it's how you smell."

She let that sink in for a little while. "You don't do much talking in a bee hive. But if you smell the right way, if you have the *hive* smell, then all is well. The bees will let you in the hive without any argument."

"That's so," said husky Apis. "There are sentries at the entrance to every hive. They're usually young and not too bright. If you smell of the hive, they let you past. Of course, if a mouse smelt of the hive, they'd let him past. If a rat did. If a possum did. They're not too bright, as I said. But—they're the only ones we can find for the job."

"Would *you* like to smell right?" asked Miss Nancy Clancy from her position on the window sill.

"Well," I said. "I'm supposed to be having an operation."

"Oh," Apis told me, "they leave people here for weeks before they touch them. We've seen children very nearly die of boredom in here. In this very ward."

Miss Nancy Clancy said, "Yes. We come down here a lot, mainly when Mrs Abey's radio breaks down. And that's what we generally see. Children dying of boredom."

"There's no reason why you shouldn't visit the hive. With us," Apis suggested. "It would be company for Miss Nancy Clancy."

"Apis would have you back," said the girl, "in time to have your appendix out, with a slight delay at Abey's for *Rick the Frontier Scout*."

I didn't feel lonely any more. My side no longer hurt, and I did *not* want to die of boredom. But I also was a little afraid of walking amongst bees who were as big as St Bernard dogs.

I heard Apis laughing in her throaty way. "I know. You think you'll be stung. It won't happen." With that she pounced on me and we tumbled over and over on the vast white plain of the hospital bed. The bee's fur tickled me. Sometimes I sneezed. I could hear Miss Nancy Clancy clapping. At last the bee stopped and I lay panting and laughing.

"There you are," said Apis. "You are now a bee of my hive. You can get past the sentries at the gateway. And inside, everyone will shake you by the hand. So to speak. Hee-yup!"

Apis squatted so that I could climb on her back. "Hang on to my armor," she said, "don't take handfuls of my hair. Miss Nancy Clancy does that."

Above us Miss Nancy Clancy muttered dreamily. "Handfuls of hair, up in the air." It was a childish rhyme, and I don't think she meant us to hear it.

"I wish you'd stop," Apis told her.

I climbed on Apis's back. Underneath her fur was a sort of coat of armor. I dug my hands into a chink in this armor. "That's right," she said. My legs dangled beside her middle legs.

And then she flew. I had never been on a ferris wheel, let alone in a plane. That flight from the bed to the window sill was the first and the best flight of my life. With a hard little clicking sound, Apis landed beside Miss Nancy Clancy. "Remember, no handfuls of hair. Here, *or* up in the air."

"As you say," said Miss Nancy Clancy. And squeezed aboard Apis's back and straight away took two handfuls of the fur on the bee's neck.

"Can't you understand plain radio talk?" the bee asked her.

"If I put my hands down in your chinks," Miss Nancy Clancy explained, "I get wax all over them."

"And I get a headache if you don't. Ned, could you hang on to Miss Nancy Clancy around the waist.

I did this.

"Easy," Nancy Clancy said.
"Not so squeezy.
It isn't good taste
To maul a lady's waist."

"God help us," said Apis and instantly flew out the window.

For a whole minute, while I clung to Apis's back, I don't think I breathed at all. It was not just that I was flying, even though that was exciting. But the outside world had changed as well. The bushes in the hospital garden now seemed taller than mountain cedars, and the gum trees themselves looked higher than any mountain I'd ever seen. Apis seemed to be flying straight for the giant black top of Doctor Morgan's Ford motor car. The sunlight flashed off the shiny paintwork of the car and blinded me. "Watch out!" I called to Apis. Now that I was bee-size, I didn't want to collide with an automobile. When I got my breath I began

laughing. Nancy Clancy looked over her shoulder at me as if she was an adult and I was a child. "You'll get used to it," she told me. "You'll settle down."

I could see the flowers in the hospital flower beds below me. They were now as big as table tops. And something else. The giant daisies below me weren't white any more. They were a strange violet.

"Hey," I called to Nancy Clancy. "The daisies are violet."

She gave a loud sigh. I could hear it above the flutter of Apis's wings. She said,

"Now you see,
like a bee.
What was once whi-olet
is now violet."

Like Apis, I was getting sick of all her rhymes. For a second, I wanted to reach out and pull one of her corkscrew curls. But I thought I'd better not do that yet. I was a guest. I needed both my hands as well.

I got used to seeing giant violet flowers where once there were small white ones. We flew along the river bank. There were gum trees with blossoms on their branches, and I could see bees as large as Apis working amongst the blossoms. Their noses were deep in the flowers, sucking up nectar. I could see the yellow pollen of the flowers caught in hairy baskets on their back legs.

"Tch, tch!" said Apis. "Some of them do seven trips a day. I don't know who they're trying to impress. First bit of cold weather in the autumn and they turn over on their backs and die from over work. I think three trips a day is enough for any sensible bee."

"Three trips to the flowers," said Nancy Clancy,

"And three trips to Mrs Abey's at radio hours."

Apis turned towards a great tree. I didn't know then that it would be my home for the summer. "See," she called. "That hole in the trunk. Straight ahead. That's home and hive."

I could see ahead of us a hole like the mouth of a cave, right there in the wood of the big mountain ash tree.

"It's perfect," Apis continued, praising her home. "See, the tree has grown so that there's a level place outside the mouth of the hive. That's where we'll land. Look, you can see the sentries there."

3

Romeo Drone and Landing

APIS STARTED BUZZING and dropped down towards the doorway of her home and its sentry bees. But before we could land another bee butted past us. Its wings brushed my leg. "Rotten drone!" said Apis.

This bee was nearly twice as big as Apis, certainly twice as fat.

"Romeo!" said Apis. "It's that Romeo."

"Romeo the drone-ee-oh!" said Nancy Clancy.

Apis stood still in the air flapping her wings, delaying our landing. "Romeo is a fat drone from another hive. He's in love with our Queen. Always trying to sneak in to see her. I hope the girls on the gate are awake."

Romeo landed on the ledge outside the doorway of the hive. At first it seemed that the sentry bees were asleep, for they let him waddle up the ledge. He was nearly through the doorway when three sentries shook themselves, and ran to stop him. They dragged and pushed at his fat body, trying to push him on his back. But he kept dragging away from them. At last two of them got their heads under his belly and lifted. The lovesick Romeo went over on his side. Two more sentries now rushed up and began to drag him by the hind legs. "Easy, easy!" we heard him say in a squawky voice.

"He watches serials too," Miss Nancy Clancy explained. "He listens to *When a Girl Marries* at Mrs Maguire's. That's what makes him carry on so stupid."

Five sentries had now pushed and pulled Romeo to the rim of the ledge. They rocked him there a few times, just like workmen getting ready to roll a rock off a cliff. Then, with one last heave-ho, they pushed him over the edge. "Oh no!" we heard him call as he fell.

We saw him fall all the way to grass. He landed with a jolt on his back. "He must be dead!" I said, feeling sorry for the fat drone.

"Him?" asked Apis and snorted. And, looking again, I saw Romeo heave himself off his back, waggle the feelers of his pleasant face, check his body all over with his front and hind legs, and fly away slowly towards his own hive.

"And don't come back!" called Apis after him.

A second later we landed on the platform from which the sentries had just slung Romeo. I was nervous at the idea of being flung off the landing as Romeo had been and I noticed Nancy Clancy was quiet too. After their success with Romeo, the sentries were very excited and came straight up to us.

"Now just relax," Apis told us. "Talk if you like. But softly."

Five sentries peered at Apis with their large eyes, then at us. They felt along Apis's back with their feelers. These feelers tickled Nancy Clancy through her dress and she laughed.

"Not so hard with those smelly feelers," she muttered, "The Clancy's are a race of squealers."

"They're smelling us *and* feeling us at the same time," Apis went on chatting as the sentries felt us all over. "We're rather luckier than some people. We can smell through our feelers. Our touchers and our sniffers aren't miles apart. As with some animals I could name."

"She means us," said Nancy Clancy, and poked her tongue out at one of the sentries, who took no notice.

"It's going to be all right," Apis went on, "because you have the right smell for our nest. Now if you didn't, the sentries would roll you over and slip a sting in you. It's different with Romeo, Romeo's just a nuisance drone, they let him go. But anyone else...You might fight them, but in the end they'd get you. In would go the sting, and in a little while, you wouldn't be breathing. Take my meaning?"

"Say you are an ant," said Nancy Clancy, "They'd really make you pant."

"They also sting people who make bad poetry," Apis said with a little laugh.

"That's a lie," the girl said.

At last the sentries decided we belonged to the hive. They backed away from us and began to frisk a returning bee who had just landed behind us.

Now Apis walked forward to the mouth of the hive. A great cave seemed to open up inside this gateway. I could at first see nothing in there. It was all dimness. But there was plenty to hear. There was loud buzzing, the flapping of wings, the clip-clop of the feet of working bees. Then my eyes got used to the dark. I saw half a dozen eager-looking bees rushing towards us. "They're the young workers," groaned Apis. "They think I've got a load of pollen and nectar. As if three loads a day isn't enough." She stared at the young bees. They seemed to frown and stand still. "Clear out!" she told them. "Clear out!"

They ran away into the dark. "That crowd doesn't know how to relax," Apis told us.

Nancy Clancy nudged me. "Look!" She pointed above her head. I looked. Rising high above us were great walls of beeswax. In the walls were doorways, some of them shut up with beeswax, some of them open. Many bees were crawling up and down these walls, walking in and out of the doorways, working in the various apartments. Because the whole thing *was* like a great apartment building, except that these apartments were not built from the ground up, but were hung from the roof! Looking up at them, I could understand why Apis was so proud of her hive.

"I'll take you straight to Miss Nancy Clancy's room," said Apis. "You're probably still tired, after that hospital."

"Where is the joy?" asked Miss Nancy Clancy. "In sharing my room with a boy?"

"You know how things are, Miss Clancy," Apis said. "We need every room we have to store food and hatch the babies in. So don't argue. Ned will stay with you."

Straight away Apis began climbing the walls of one of the apartments houses. Now I really had to hang on. I hugged her plump waist to stop myself from slipping off her back and falling to the bottom of the hive.

Apis stopped at a cell door that was like all the other cell doors.

"Here we are," she said.

All the apartments or cells we had passed were six-sided. This might have suited bees, but I knew it would not suit Nancy Clancy and me. As Apis tumbled us into Nancy Clancy's cell I saw that the girl had a feather bed with legs of different lengths to fit the strange floor. She had a table and chair cut the same way. On the table stood a candle and some old-fashioned children's books.

4

One Hundred and Twenty Year Old Girl

"If you'll excuse me," said the bee, after I'd had a good stare at Miss Clancy's apartment, "I think I'll go and rest. Just be careful though with that candle."

Now Miss Nancy Clancy and I were alone. She pulled out her chair, sat on it, took one of her old-fashioned books and began to read. I sat on the bed.

After a while I said, "What's the name of the book?"

"*The Butterfly Ball and the Grasshopper's Feast,*" she said.

"What's it like?"

"Boring. I've been reading it for a hundred and ten years."

"Did you say *a hundred and ten years?*"

"I did."

"That's not true."

"How would you know?" she asked me, lifting her head proudly.

"No one's a child for a hundred and ten years."

"You are suggesting I'm a liar?" she asked me, slamming the book down with a bang.

Before I could answer, a strange bee poked it's head into Miss Nancy Clancy's apartment. "Dinner time," said the girl. She picked up an old china cup that stood beside her books. She walked to the bee. From the end of its nose hung a great golden glob. Miss Nancy Clancy neatly collected it in her cup, bowed to the bee, who then disappeared, and walked back to her chair. She began to feed herself the golden food with a spoon. "This is food and this is drink. This is royal jelly. You can have a little even if you do think I'm a liar."

I ate it and it was wonderful.

"They feed the babies on that," said Nancy Clancy. "They think we're babies, that's why they feed it to us. When they're raising a baby to be queen, they feed her nothing else."

"Why don't you talk in rhymes any more?" I asked her.

"Oh, I only do that to annoy Apis."

Just then a further bee appeared at Miss Clancy's doorway. This one had a ball of purple and gold held in its front legs. Seeing it, Miss Nancy jumped up and waved her arms. "No thanks, no thanks, no thanks!"

At last the bee shook its head and vanished.

"They think we need pollen too," she told me. "Can you imagine sitting up eating a ball of pollen? Ugh!"

I ate up the royal jelly quickly. When it was all gone I felt tired. I yawned. "But you *aren't* a hundred and ten years old."

"Actually, I'm a hundred and twenty," said Nancy. "I didn't take to this hive-life till I was ten years old." Before I could go on arguing, we had yet another visitor. This time it was Apis. It was easy to tell her slightly shaggier hair, her soft eyes, the shape of her head from those of the young workers who had fed us earlier.

"Excuse me," she said. "Does Ned know there is a bucket at the rear of this apartment in case he needs...?"

"Oh," said Miss Nancy Clancy. "If he thinks I'm not the age I say, I'll ban him from the toilet for a year and a day. You see, my dear bee friend, this boy doesn't believe that I'm a hundred and twenty years old. And whoever doesn't believe I'm a hundred and twenty years old, doesn't believe I'm Nancy Clancy."

"She's Nancy Clancy," said Apis. "And she's a hundred and twenty years old. Please sleep well, my friends. Goodnight."

When Apis had gone again, Nancy Clancy went to her table, and lifted the book called *The Butterfly Ball and the Grasshopper's Feast*. She showed the first page to me. *By William Roscoe*, it said. And underneath, *London, 1807*.

She could see I was very surprised. "I'll tell you my story," said Miss Nancy Clancy. "Unless it's likely to bore you."

"No, no," I rushed to say, "I don't get bored."

A hundred and ten years ago (said Miss Nancy Clancy), when I was ten years old, I came into this valley with my father. There was no one here then. We had a cart that was dragged by four oxen. My father had three horses, and a black man to show him the way. I didn't have a mother, she died while I was a baby. A lot of mothers died in those days. My father was a very quiet man because he missed my mother. His only friend was the black man who brought us here. Are you interested yet or will I stop?

All right, you're interested. One very hot day we were traveling along the banks of this river, this very river, the one you can see from the mouth of the hive. We stopped at midday and my father's black friend started a fire and baked some bread in the ashes. Then we all lay down under the wagon to rest. There were lots of bees along the river banks gathering pollen and nectar, even then. Soon my father and his black friend were asleep, but the bees kept me awake. I got up. I tried to read my books. Even that very book there I just showed you, *The Butterfly Ball.* But it wasn't any use. So, with a book under each arm, I decided to go for a walk. And that's how it all started.

Now do you still want me to go on? I can see you do.

All right. I went walking up into the hills. There were lots of trees, gum trees and mountain ash, and soon I couldn't see the wagon any more. Half-way up the hill, I saw a fat black snake. It had a red belly. As soon as it saw me it ran away. I thought, Nancy Clancy—the great scarer of snakes.

After a while I could tell it was time to go back to the wagon. I could tell it was about time my father and the black man would be stirring. But when I came downhill again and out of the trees, the whole river bank looked different. I'd come out at the wrong place.

So I sat down on the river bank and waited for my father to come for me. All afternoon passed and he didn't come. Then the sun went down behind the hills. No, I didn't cry. Well, maybe a tear, or two. Children will be children, you know. I hid in the trees that night in case any of the black tribes came along the river. They like little girls with curly hair, you know. It's said that black tribes-people used sometimes to take away little white children just because of their curly hair. I didn't want that to happen to me, even though I like people to admire my hair.

The next morning, as the sun came up, that old black snake with the red belly came back and sat on a rock and looked at me. I clapped my hands, but this time he didn't blink. That old black snake wasn't scared of Nancy Clancy any more.

Then I walked up the river and down the river looking for my father. I got so hungry. I called. Where could he have got to? I still don't know the answer to that. A hundred and ten years, and I still don't know.

In the afternoon I climbed the hill again. I thought I might be able to see the wagon from on top of the hill there. I was so hungry. I sat down under a big blue gum and cried first, yes I cried, I don't mind admitting it, and then I slept.

When I woke up, there were black people all around me. Black men with spears, black women with wooden dishes on one hip and a little black child on the other. I thought, here we go! They're going to keep me prisoner for my curls. I tried to stand up and run, but my legs were too weak. I had been lost a day and a half, and had had nothing to eat. So two young black women came and helped me up, not roughly, and helped me along as the tribe marched downhill and along the river.

In the last light of that day, the men started spearing eels in the river, and the women cooked them. Young boys made little shelters out of the bark from trees, and young girls put the roots of plants on a flat stone and pounded them to a flour with other stones held in their hands. They gave me eel and some of this flour to eat. But that night it was so cold.

The next morning the tribe took me with them. But I felt weak and one of the young black women had to carry me. In the night a plump black woman slept beside me to keep me warm. But the cold was stronger than the plump woman. When I remember how cold it was, and how I kept waking and weeping, I feel sad for the little girl I was then. Yes, sad. Because I was only ten years old then, no older than you.

And it started raining—you know the way it rains in this valley. The tribe did not go on walking the next morning. The plump woman and I snuggled together in a little bark shelter. I didn't want to eat anything she gave me. I wanted to be warm and sleep without waking up again.

The plump woman and the other tribes-people were very worried about me now. When the rain stopped and the sun came out, they propped me up against a tree trunk so that I could get warm in the sunlight. But I kept sleeping and woke only one more time. The sun was going down behind the hill and I could see a bee walking up my chest with a drop of golden liquid for me on her tongue. You know how it was, the same thing happened to you in hospital, didn't it?

(I nodded. I thought Miss Nancy Clancy's story was the strangest I'd ever heard.)

The bee's name was Cilla (Miss Nancy Clancy continued) and she felt sorry for me. I told her I didn't want her feeling sorry for me. I didn't want the sympathy of a bee. But she kept on feeling sorry and I couldn't do anything to stop her. She said she'd given me the golden drop because I wasn't going to see my father ever again. It was some sort of charity for losing your relatives. I called her a liar when she said that. But I knew she was telling the truth.

She said that I could come and spend summer with her and at the end of the summer she would put me somewhere warm where I could sleep all winter. If she herself should die during the winter, she would leave a message with a young bee so that I would be collected in the spring and brought as a guest to the hive.

And that's what's been happening for a hundred and ten years (said Miss Nancy Clancy) and I must say it's very pleasant and I've met lots of bees.

I frowned and felt a deep fright as I heard the end of Miss Nancy Clancy's story.

"The same thing happened to me as to you," I said. "A bee crawled up my chest. Does that mean I'm never going to see my mother and father again?"

"Don't be silly. It's an entirely different case."

"But I was in the hospital, and Apis crawled up my chest with a drop of golden liquid on her tongue..."

"It doesn't mean you're not going to see your mamma again, babykins. Apis is just sentimental, that's all. From listening to all those serials. She didn't say anything about your mother and father, did she?"

"No."

"There you are. That shows you. Now let's go to sleep."

"Where do I sleep?"

"Across the foot of my bed," she told me, as if I was a pup.

"What will I do for sheets and covers?"

"You won't have any need of covers. It's a hot night."

And Miss Nancy Clancy was right. All night, whenever I woke, I could hear the flutter of bees' wings in the hive. Some of the young workers stayed up all night fanning the rest of us, keeping us cool. That sound made me feel cozy and safe, and before long I went into a deep sleep out of which I did not come until morning.

5

Ned Kelly Meets the Queen

IT'S MORNING, said Nancy Clancy, shaking my elbow. "I've been up half an hour practicing my rhymes."

"Oh," I said. I sat up, dangling my legs over the end of Miss Nancy Clancy's bed. I still wasn't certain where I was, and my head felt put on crooked, as your head often does when you first wake up.

"Cheer up," she told me. "You'll probably see the Queen today." Then she frowned. She had thought of something that had nothing to do with beehives and early morning. "I wonder why people say cheer up instead of cheer down. Consider this, if you're not cheerful you're upset and if you're *upset* then you should cheer *down.* Don't you think?"

"If you like," I sighed. I wasn't in the mood for arguing. I was missing my mother and father.

"All right," Miss Nancy Clancy decided. "From now on we both cheer down." Before I had any chance to cheer down, two bees appeared at the doorway of the apartment. One carried a bead of royal jelly, the other a drop of water which looked like a jewel in the hive's dim light. Nancy Clancy ran to collect both the jelly and the water in the cups. She handed both cups to me and I began to eat the jelly and drink the water, but slowly.

"Come on, eat up!" she said. "Though that's another ridiculous phrase of course. How can you eat *up* when the food travels down from your mouth to your stomach?" I was feeling better now and so I began to discuss the question with her.

"You pick it *up* from the plate or the cup to eat it," I explained.

"Well in that case you can pick up but eat down. That's what we'll say from now on."

"You can say it. I won't."

"All right," she said, sniffing and turning her face away. "If you want to be as stupid as all other humans, you go ahead eating up. I'll eat down and I'll cheer down, and when you're a hundred and twenty years like me, you'll see I was right."

At this point of the argument Apis poked her head round the edge of the cell.

"Good morning," she said in her husky voice.

"Good morning to you, faithful bee," Nancy Clancy replied. "And what have you got to show to we?"

"Well, if you both hurry we can see the Queen go by."

Nancy Clancy rushed me to the cell door and we looked down. Below us a beautiful bee, much bigger than Apis, much longer than Romeo the drone, was swaying slowly across the wall of honeycomb. Other bees, workers and servants, guards and fanning bees to keep her cool, crowded around her, touching her gently, fanning and fussing. She walked more gracefully than a racehorse or any other animal I had ever seen. Her waist was thinner than the waist on the models in the front window of Murphy's dress shop, and her wings, which were no bigger than Apis's wings, were folded over her back.

"She's on her way to lay eggs," Apis explained. "But she might have a moment to meet you."

Apis left us, climbed down the wall, dragged two young fanning bees away from the Queen by their hind legs, and rushed into the empty space at the Queen's side. We could see the Queen and Apis talking, touching each other gently with their feelers. Then Apis turned away and led the Queen up the wall towards us.

I felt nervous and started combing my hair with my fingers. When Apis was close to us again she whispered, "If you talk in rhymes, Miss Clancy, I promise I'll sting you."

At last the Queen stood at the door, her feelers swaying gracefully and her beautiful molten eyes looking at us. Apis coughed. "Her Majesty decided to come and visit you only because you aren't good at climbing up and down the honeycomb."

"I'm all right at it," Nancy Clancy muttered. She pointed to me. "But my friend isn't yet accustomed to it."

Apis coughed again. "This, your Majesty, is Miss Nancy Clancy whom you already know, and this is Ned. Ned and Nancy, Queen Selma."

"What would you like me to say, you two?" Queen Selma asked in a slightly cracked voice.

I was surprised to find she could talk just the same as Apis, and my mouth must have hung open for a second. The Queen noticed it, laughed, and began talking fast.

"Oh yes," she said, "my good friend Apis has taught me how to talk radio. I can say, *Good morning, children*, like Mrs Martin in *Martin's Corner*. I can say, *Hullo, white children!* like the little black boy in *The Search for the Golden Boomerang*, or I can say *G'day, kids* like Dave in *Dad and Dave*. Which would you prefer to hear?"

I was speechless as Selma rattled off the names of radio shows, but Miss Nancy Clancy was able to say, "I think I'd like to hear *Good morning, children*."

"All right," said the Queen. "*Good morning, children!*"

"Good morning, Your Majesty," Nancy Clancy sang, bowing as low as she could on the crooked floor.

"Now," said Queen Selma, looking at me with large black eyes, "I have to ask this young man some questions, grill him, get him to come clean. Miss Nancy Clancy tells me that when she was young there was a queen called Victoria who never laid any eggs. Is she still alive?"

"No," I said. "No, Queen Victoria died a long time ago."

"Of course," Selma sniffed. "No one wants a queen who doesn't lay eggs."

I thought it wouldn't be polite to tell the beautiful Selma that humans never expected Queen Victoria to lay eggs.

"Enjoy your stay then," said Queen Selma. "And, as they say in *Rick the Frontier Scout, I'm gonna head down that there canyon.* Good morning."

She waved her feelers especially gracefully, turned and swayed away, and all the fanners and escort bees fell in at her side, marching sideways, keeping her company.

6

Selma Lays a Queen Egg

WATCHING THE QUEEN go, Apis seemed thoughtful. If a bee can do such a thing as frown, I would have said she was frowning. Then she shook herself and turned towards me.

"It's time you learnt to get around the hive on your own," she told me. I thought of the great wall of cells and apartments in which Nancy Clancy and I sat. I thought of all the other walls of beeswax that made up the hive. Did she really expect me to climb up and down them? Did royal jelly turn you into a hive climber?

"Quite right," Nancy Clancy said. "You can't get round on Apis's back all day. She has enough to do."

"Keep your elbows loose," Apis advised me, wriggling her own front elbows. "Ready, Miss Clancy?"

Miss Clancy said,

"Lead on, brave bee
I'll climb each wall
Never will Nancy Clancy fall."

"Sometimes I wish you would fall," Apis remarked and stepped back from the door to let us climb out backwards.There was something about the way *I* backed out the door that made her chuckle.

We seemed to be on a newly built part of the hive and all the apartments stood wide open. So I had to climb all spread out, like a crab. I kept feeling for places to put my feet and hands. In fact my hands sweated from the fear I was suffering. Helpfully, Apis called, "A little to the right with your left foot. That's right. A little to the left with your right foot."

When you look at a honeycomb it seems so smooth, but I found that all over it there were tiny cracks where my hands and feet fitted. Within five minutes I began to feel more comfortable, climbing down that dim wall.

"This way," Apis called. "But watch out for the crowds. They don't look where they're going."

Soon we *were* amongst crowds of bees. I lost all sense of danger now and looked around me. Some bees were working on new cells. They seemed to take sheets of wax from the cracks in their armor, knead them into the shape they wanted with their front legs and feelers, cut them neatly with their mouths and put them in place to make a part of a wall. They were quick and they were neat and all their angles were right.

"The wax!" I called to Apis. "The wax comes from the bodies of the bees?" I had never known that before.

"Where did you think?" asked Nancy Clancy in her haughty way. "The wax factory?"

"Look," Apis called. "Below us. Queen Selma is laying." I looked down, feeling a little giddy at first. All I could see was a great mass of bees. It would be a little time before I'd find out all the secrets of the hive, how the honey and pollen were stored, how the young were made.

Queen Selma—I found out—surrounded by all her fanners and escorts, would lay many eggs a day in the early summer. Some of the eggs would grow into workers and others into drones like Romeo, the lovesick male bee we had met the day before.

Soon each egg in its own cell would hatch and a little grub-like creature would lie there. Nursemaids fed it royal jelly for a few days and, when it began to change into a small insect, gave it plenty of pollen and honey and walled up the entrance to its cell. It wasn't a thick wall they made to lock the babies in. It had holes in it to let the air through. The little insect would eat up all its supplies till it was a full-grown young bee. Then it would chew its way out of its cell. If it was a worker, it started work within a few days, and if a drone, it lay around and was fed as the drones always were.

At the bottom of the wall where Apis and Nancy Clancy and I were climbing that morning were some strange cells that hung downwards and were shaped like ice-cream cones. I could tell that Selma's escorts were trying to force her to lay eggs in them, and that she didn't want to and tried to walk away from them. The escort bees however pushed her towards them, crowding her, making her back until the rear half of her body was inside one of the cone cells. When she had laid an egg in that cell, they forced her on to the next.

"Why?" I asked Apis.

"Well," said Apis. She didn't seem to want to tell me. "The eggs she's laying *there*, in *those* cells...they'll be raised as queens. Fed on a pure diet of royal jelly and brought up to rule. Selma doesn't want to lay queen cells, no queen does."

"Why?" I persisted.

"Because Selma's frightened she might have to go away from the hive and leave it for some young and beautiful queen to take over."

I still hadn't finished asking questions. "But are they making her lay queen eggs?"

Apis kept quiet for half a minute, looking at me, still wondering if she should tell me. "Well," she said at last, "a queen has a sort of sweetness all over her body, and when we touch the queen we taste the sweetness, and when we pass nectar or honey to each other, the sweetness is passed on. But when the hive gets crowded or the queen gets older, there isn't enough queen sweetness to go around. And Selma's getting old and Selma"—by now Apis was whispering—"Selma doesn't have enough sweetness. And so she's been forced to lay eggs in those cells, the queen cells. Do you understand that?"

I nodded.

"Then keep it a secret," she warned me. "In about seventeen days one of those new queens will be ready to be born. And then everything will be turned upside down."

I got so brave on that wall that after a time I was able to look over my shoulder and see what was happening on the wall opposite ours. I noticed that already workers were flying into the hive from the outside world carrying pollen in the baskets on their back legs and nectar in their mouths. When they landed, young bees rushed up to them, unpacked the pollen from the baskets, and rushed to store it in one or another of the cells. Other young bees took the nectar from them and stretched it out on their long tongues and packed it in one cell and then in another, helping it to dry and become honey. But the royal jelly which Selma and the babies were fed was never stored in cells. The bees carried it in their bodies and when they needed it for feeding the Queen or the young, there it would suddenly be, a golden drop on the end of their tongues.

I watched the young workers walling up any cells that were full of honey, molding and cutting the wax, molding and cutting quickly. Apis in turn watched me. "Oh yes," she said, "they work hard."

I wondered why Apis didn't have to work as hard as they did. Because she taught the Queen to speak as they do on the radio? Or because she had visitors? Nancy Clancy and me.

"Don't look now," shouted Nancy Clancy,
"But right below
Is Razzle-
Dazzle Basil."

"The idiot!" said Apis.

In a space inside the front door, a group of drones was meeting in a bunch. They were husky fellows and I noticed their large eyes that took up almost all their head. One of them stood apart from the others and seemed to be making a speech. When he saw us he began to speak in English, as if to impress us.

"And, gentlemen, I would like to draw your attention to our two young visitors from the outside world. I would like in their presence to ask, are our so-called *sisters*, the so-called *workers*, going to throw us out of the hive again this autumn? Are they going to do it in front of the eyes of two strangers from the outside world, two such persons as those climbing on the comb there? Are they really going to shock those young eyes by hurling us, sad, solitary, sopping and starving, out into a forest full of enemies? When we try to return, are they going to hurl us once more away from the door and tell us there is no room or food for us? Does the race of humans treat each other like that? Do they behave like that in *Martin's Corner* or *Rick the Frontier Scout?* I say that we belong here as much as the workers, as much even as the Queen!"

This idea appealed to the drones. They waved their feelers at Basil, applauding him.

"My cry," said Basil, "is *Power to the Drones!*"

This really made them crazy. Some of them fell over with excitement.

"Do you really throw them out when the rains come in the autumn?" I asked Apis.

She tossed her head. "Basil's an idiot," she said again. Then, "Do you want to come out with me?"

Nancy Clancy answered for both of us. "Certainly we want to go out, bee, to gather nectar, the basis of hon-ey."

Straight away, Apis let go of the wall and hovered near Nancy and me, flapping her wings up and down but floating, not moving forward. "Jump on!" she yelled. "And once again, Miss Clancy, no hair pulling!"

7

Giving Romeo the Hive-Smell

We flew out into the clear day, past the guards and the fanners at the door. Circling, we saw the river and flew over the cow paddocks. I kept thinking that the cows would be so surprised to see me, Ned, a fourth grader, flying overhead in a valley in which few planes were ever seen. But they kept their heads down, eating grass in the strange bunch-lipped way cows have.

We arrived amongst a stand of spotted gum trees. They were in blossom, and thousands of bees were working all around us. In the fork of one of the trees, Apis set us down. From this place, we could see a barge in the river carrying timber, and a man fishing from a row-boat. Then Apis went to work with the other bees.

"Don't fidget," Nancy Clancy advised me as we sat there. "If you fidget you attract birds. Some birds eat bees, you know. So they'd certainly eat us. Haven't you heard of birds called honey-eaters? Well, they eat bees as well."

Of course I sat very still and didn't even speak. I looked around the sky for possible winged gobblers of me. A few magpies flew amongst the spotted gum branches and went on their way. Cockatoos went past cackling and making for the river.

"Well, you don't have to be absolutely silent," Nancy Clancy said next.

Nothing I did seemed to please her. She spoke to me the way schoolchildren speak to the very young.

"Why do you talk so bossy?" I asked her.

Her voice softened a little. "I just didn't want you to think every bird was going to gobble you up."

We watched the bees putting their heads in the blossoms, to search out the nectar from deep inside, to suck it up and store it inside themselves. We watched them pack the pollen into their baskets. But after a while, I got drowsy.

I was nearly asleep when there was a blur in front of my eyes and Romeo, the fat drone, landed with a plop beside us.

"Hullo," he said in a shy and squeaky little voice that sounded strange, coming from such a hefty body.

"Hullo," I said, but Nancy only nodded.

"How are you getting on," he asked, "in beautiful Selma's hive?"

"Listen Romeo," said Nancy, "we all like you. You're nicer than that fool Basil. But really, it isn't any use your hanging around Selma. She mated with a drone long ago, and she won't be mating again. And the place is full of drones as it is..."

"Oh, I don't want to mate with her. I want to be her servant. I want to help guard her. I want to wag my wings and make her hive cool. I want to be her knight."

Nancy giggled behind her hand at the idea of *Sir* Romeo.

"I'm an expert in the area of knights," said Romeo. "I keep well instructed by listening to the radio. I've heard all about knights and ladies and how the knight was faithful to the lady even if she never let him make love to her." He sighed. "I heard all about it in a radio program called *The Knights of Pentagel*."

"*Pentagel?*" giggled Nancy. "Sounds like something you take for a sore belly."

"I was thinking," Romeo coughed. "If I got into her hive I could be her knight. Oh she's beautiful. She's as beautiful as leather, and her eyes are broad and beautiful, and she has three golden rings round her body..."

"And her voice is scratchy," said cruel Nancy Clancy.

"And her voice is..." went on Romeo in a dream. "No...no, I wouldn't say that, Miss Clancy, her voice isn't scratchy. Oh no." He coughed again, just like someone acting on the radio. "I can never get past those guard bees. They let other drones past. But I suppose I'm the kind of person other people like to push and shove. I thought that if we all had a wrestle together, nothing rough, then I'd get the right smell for the hive and your guards would get confused and let me in."

"I don't know if it's right for us to do that," said Nancy Clancy primly. "After all, we're guests of the hive."

"I was wondering too," Romeo went on, "if I could stay with you and the young gentleman here until I get used to the hive and meet Queen Selma?"

It was the first time anyone had called me a "young gentleman." The only gentlemen in our town were bank managers and doctors and teachers. I began to feel kindly towards poor Romeo.

"We could fit him in," I said to Miss Nancy Clancy. "He could sleep in the back of the cell."

"You forget," Miss Nancy Clancy sniffed. "It's *my* cell. And look at his size."

"You can wrestle with me, Romeo," I told the poor fat drone.

"Mind you, not rough," he pleaded.

"How are you going to be a knight if you're afraid to wrestle?" the girl asked him. But Romeo and I had already begun, tussling and rolling in the wide fork of that tree. Romeo gave little yelps and grunts whenever I grabbed one of his legs. He was a very gentle fellow, and I was enjoying myself.

At last, Miss Clancy joined in and she wrestled harder than either of us. It's always surprising how tough some girls can be, and I could tell even by the way Miss Clancy pulled her sleeves up before diving on top of us that she was one of the tough ones.

The three of us were struggling and whooping, when we heard Apis land with a plop beside us. In the long hairs of her hind legs she carried lumps of pollen, food for the hive. She wasn't happy with us.

"What's this?" she said. "You look like a choice ball of caterpillar all tangled up. It's a wonder some large bird hasn't eaten you."

We all became still as we thought of the savage beaks of magpies. And then I began to tell her what we had been doing for Romeo.

"It's nonsense," she said. She seemed only ever to be really angry with drones. "Romeo, I don't know who's a bigger lunatic, that Basil or you." "Please," said fat Romeo in his tiny voice. "I'm sick of being thrown out by those guards. It isn't the bruises. It's the way I've become a public joke that upsets me."

Apis raised her voice. "Do you expect me, a worker, loaded down with nectar and pollen, to care whether you're a public joke or not?"

"The boy said I could go with you."

Apis stared at me. I was frightened of her for the first time, for there was no softness in her eye any more. "Did you? Well, I don't care what happens either way. But since you invited him, Ned, you can ride home to the hive on *his* back. You may have noticed, I have enough to carry as it is. Oh yes, you'll get past the guards now. You have the right smell. But remember that I said no good will come of it. Remember that. Come, Miss Clancy."

Nancy Clancy climbed primly aboard Apis's back.

"The experts say it's good for health," she sang, "to have the whole bee's back to oneself."

They flew away. I climbed slowly onto Romeo's back, he gathered himself and lunged forward into free air. It wasn't like flying with Apis. Romeo wheezed and bumped up and down in the summer air like one of those old airplanes they brought to the valley for the Agricultural Show. It was a long journey home. The smallest draught of wind would blow the drone off course. I imagined myself falling off Romeo's plump back and being snatched up by a hungry cow and slowly chewed.

At last I saw the door of the hive and the guard bees pacing. "I go forward for my lady queen," Romeo called grandly to me over his shoulder. "Without hesitation, without turning back."

And so we landed right amongst the strong young guard bees. Three ran straight at us. You could see they almost remembered Romeo as a person who should be thrown out of the hive, but when they felt him they found he had the right smell, the right passport, the same one I had. And so they stood back and let us through. Romeo waddled into the hive, laughing with joy.

Beyond the guards, Apis and Miss Clancy were waiting for us. "Well! said Apis. But before she could say anything else, six young bees marching in two lines of three each came out from deep inside the hive. Between them they carried the body of a dead worker, its legs crossed crookedly over its body. Everyone was silent while the funeral procession went past. When the carriers of the dead bee got to the mouth of the hive, they let go of it. It was carried away by the breeze.

"I knew her," said Apis, looking at Romeo. "That's what happens to workers. They slave and they die slaving. They have no time for sentimental nonsense."

Romeo shrugged. "It isn't my fault," he said.

"Anyhow," Apis continued, "I have to do another load if I want to be up at Mrs Abey's in time for *When a Girl Marries*."

We all began to laugh at her then, even Romeo, at the idea of her saying she was a slave when she had time to listen to radio programs.

"All right," she said, a smile in her voice, "you can all come too."

8

Maurie Abey Hates Insects

APIS FETCHED ANOTHER load of pollen and nectar back to the hive, and then, a little before eleven o'clock, we all flew uphill to Mrs Abey's old wood-frame house and sat just inside her window sill. It was pleasant there. A jacaranda tree threw its shade over us, and we were pleased about that, for it was a hot morning and, back at the hive, the fanning bees had been fanning madly to keep the bee-city cool.

From our perch at the kitchen window we saw Mrs Abey come into the room, fill a kettle and put it on the wood stove. She was a sad-looking woman with brown hair. I thought I knew why she looked sad—she had a monster of a son, called Maurie Abey. Once he'd tried to run me down with his bicycle. Another time he broke the headmaster's window with an air-gun. He was always being sent home from school with notes from his teachers saying something like "Dear Mrs Abey, Your son happens to be a monster. Yours sincerely, the Teacher."

Mrs Abey turned on the radio. There was an advertisement for Valley Ice Cream and then the slow, sugary music that introduced the valley's favorite morning program—*When A Girl Marries.* When Mrs Abey was a girl and got married, she didn't know she'd give birth to something like Maurie!

"*When A Girl Marries,*" said the voice of the radio announcer. "For those who are in love and for those who remember." Romeo sighed and settled himself even more comfortably.

"When we last saw Beth," the radio went on, "she was sobbing in her room after hearing from her friend Sally that her boyfriend Kevin had invited Cathy, a newcomer to town, to the Farmers' Ball..."

And so the program went on. Beth sobbed a great deal because she really liked Kevin, in fact even loved him, and she never thought that he'd ask a strange girl called Cathy to the Farmers' Ball.

Through all the weeping and screaming of the serial, Mrs Abey just drank her tea and listened. We could have danced on the window sill and she wouldn't have noticed. Once she muttered, "That's men for you."

As the episode continued, we began to find out that the stranger Cathy was Kevin's cousin and he'd only asked her because he'd got his dates mixed and thought that his beloved Beth would be in Sydney at the time of the Ball. Just then Beth's uncle Robert was knocked down by a truck and seriously injured, and all thought of Kevin was driven from her mind. She ran into the street just as the episode ended. And as the final music played... there in the doorway was the terrible Maurie Abey with a note in his hand.

"Ma," he said, "they sent me home again."

"Oh no," said Mrs Abey. "Not again, Maurie."

"That Mrs Sayle. She picks on me."

Mrs Abey switched off the radio and, taking the note, read it. "Oh Maurie," she said, "Mrs Sayle says you gave her horse poisonous weed to eat."

"It won't kill it," said Maurie. "Not that old horse."

He crossed the room, grabbed a glass and began to pour himself water. We all watched him closely. The drama of poor Mrs Abey and her frightful son interested us as much as any radio serial.

But as Maurie stood up to drink, he saw us. "There are bloody insects all over this window sill," he said.

"Don't talk like that, son."

"Well there are!"

He picked up a copy of the *Valley News*, rolled it up to make a good insect squasher, and advanced on us.

"Quick!" called Miss Nancy Clancy and Apis, both at once. Nancy jumped on Apis's back and I on Romeo's just as he was raising his fat self to his feet. Nancy and Apis had already flown out of the window before Romeo was even properly on his legs. I saw the great roll of newspaper raised above us. "Ah—ah—ah!" was all I could say. Maurie Abey's newspaper squasher came down and hit the sill so close to us that the sound filled my head and knocked me crooked on the drone's back. I think though that the breeze it made was what lifted Romeo off the window sill and got him airborne. In a second we were flying bumpily over Mrs Abey's washing line. "Oh—oh—oh," Romeo was groaning. "That noise! Did you ever hear such a noise?"

I couldn't answer him. I saw that above us flew Apis and Miss Clancy, and Miss Clancy waved at us. Without meaning to, I began crying.

"What's the matter?" puffed Romeo in sympathy as he flapped homeward.

"I want to send a message to my mother and father. They won't know where I am."

"Oh," said Romeo gently. "Oh, of course. Don't cry, Ned."

I suppose it was the shock of being swatted by a Maurie Abey grown to a giant size that kept the tears rolling down my face and made me wonder why I had taken so long to think of home.

9

Miss Such's Typewriter

"WE COULD SEND a telegram," said Romeo.

We were all crowded—Apis, Miss Nancy Clancy, Romeo and I—into Miss Nancy Clancy's cell, and everyone was discussing my problem. "You *do* want to stay with us a little longer?" Apis asked.

I nodded. "But I don't think I'll go to Abey's again."

"Neither will I," said Romeo.

"I don't like that Maurie Abey," I explained. "He's...he's never been any better than that."

"We could send a telegram," Romeo repeated. He had probably heard of telegrams only on the radio. But I knew we couldn't walk into a Post Office and ask the postal clerk to take down a telegram. If he saw us he wouldn't believe us, and we had nothing to pay him with. Telegrams were luxuries in that town and cost a lot. "Miss Such," I said, half to myself.

"I beg your pardon?" said Romeo.

"Miss Such is a teacher at the school. She's young, no more than about twenty-one."

"How charming," Miss Nancy Clancy said bitingly. "How disarming. What has it got to do with tele...with what Romeo says?"

"She owns a typewriter," I told them.

They looked blankly at me. I explained. "You make letters by pressing the keys down. You can write to people that way. Each key has a different letter on it." I sighed. "The only trouble is, we need lots of weight to press the keys down."

Again Romeo coughed in his shy way. "Would two of us be heavy enough? Or three of us? Or four? If I sat on a key and Apis sat on top of me—now don't toss your head, Miss Apis, I won't give you a disease—and the two of you sat on Apis's back, would that work, would that make a letter, would it?"

I remembered that one afternoon Miss Such had asked me to help her carry some music books to her house in Elbow Street. As a reward she let me play with the typewriter for a few minutes. I remembered it was a heavy machine and you really had to press the keys. I remembered too that there was a bar you had to press to make a space between words, and a lever to push for a new line.

"I think we'd need more weight than that. I think we'd need more bees—more people—than just the four of us."

"Basil!" said Apis. "Let's ask Basil. He's fat and ugly enough for a job like that."

From the doorway of Miss Nancy Clancy's apartment, we could see Basil and some of the other drones still bunched together inside the hive entrance.

"Come on," said Apis. Romeo rose with a sigh and we all began climbing slantwise down the walls of cells and apartments. Close to where Basil stood there was a place where the wall met the floor. Our feet touched the bottom of the hive there, and the sound made Basil turn.

"Good afternoon," said Apis. I was surprised how sweet she sounded, because I knew she didn't like Basil. "I'd like to introduce Romeo to you. He might be of some use to your organization."

Romeo looked shy but Basil shook him heartily by the feelers. "What can I do for you, mate?" he asked.

"Well," said Romeo, "we have our young friend here, Ned, and he's just had a nasty experience. I mean, someone tried to swat us. Missed by a whisker, so to speak. Now he needs some help so that he can send a message to his hive, I mean his family. He needs a dozen sturdy drones to help him make the message on a typewriter."

Basil said nothing.

"It isn't hard work," Romeo rushed to say. "We need your weight, that's all."

"That's very well, sport," said Basil, man to man. "What do our friends here offer us in return? I mean, will *they* promise not to throw us out of the hive when the autumn rains come?"

"How can I promise that?" said Apis. "I'm just one humble worker."

"*We'll* talk to the Queen," Nancy Clancy suddenly promised. "Ned and I—if you help us—we'll talk to the Queen about not throwing you out in the autumn."

Basil shrugged. "I suppose that's fair enough. Let me talk to the boys." He turned to the other drones and buzzed and fluttered at them, giving them orders. One very plump drone began tiptoeing away and Basil dragged him back by the hind legs.

"All right," Basil said to us at last. "I can lend you a half dozen of my best lads. And myself."

"Thank you so much," said Apis sweetly.

Basil giggled. "Lead the way," he said.

The sun was only a little way above the mountains as we flew down Elbow Street. "Here, here!" I yelled when we came to the trellis gate of Miss Such's place, and we all turned left and settled on the frame of the partly opened window of the school teacher's living room.

"Sshh!" Miss Nancy Clancy told Basil and the other drones as they too landed. For Miss Such was in the room and so was young Doctor Morgan, who had treated me in the hospital so long ago. Or had it been only yesterday? Anyhow I lay flat on the window frame. Doctor Morgan was sitting in an armchair looking pale, as if he himself might be sick.

Miss Such said, "I can't face it, Ben. I can't face being a doctor's wife in a little town for the rest of my life. It doesn't mean I don't like you. You're a fine person, a much better person than I am. But Ben, I want to write books, I want to travel. Here I am, twenty-one years old, and I haven't even been to Queensland. I want to climb the Andes in South America and sail down the Nile in Egypt and see England and Ireland and travel in Japan and China. If I marry you I know I won't do any of those things, I'll have children. I know it's selfish to say that. If I had any man's children, I'd like to have yours. But that's it. Please don't, please don't ask me again."

"But I love you," Doctor Morgan said in a strangled voice.

"This is better that the radio!" Romeo whispered at my side.

"Please Ben!" said Miss Such.

They stayed silent for a while. One of Basil's drones began to buzz, but they didn't notice that.

"Do you still want me to take you to the dance tonight?" Doctor Morgan asked the schoolteacher.

"Of course. If that's what *you* want." Miss Such stood up, went to Doctor Morgan and kissed him on the forehead. Romeo sighed loudly. Then the doctor and the teacher left the room together and a few seconds later we heard the front door close.

"I think she's very sensible," said Apis. "Freedom over slavery, any day."

I was already looking at Miss Such's typewriter. There was a fresh page in it with only a line or two already typed. I climbed on Romeo's back, Miss Nancy Clancy climbed on Apis's and we flew down to Miss Such's desk, Basil's drones following us.

"This is the machine," I told Nancy and Apis, Romeo and Basil when we all stood before it. "Miss Nancy, this bar here has to be pressed whenever we need to make a space between words. When I tell you, please sit on it and pretend you're on a seesaw. Apis and Romeo, that lever there has to be pushed every time we want a new line. I'll tell you when that is. I'll call out, *Apis and Romeo, push*! Basil, you and your men will put your weight on these keys, one at a time, the ones that I tell you to, when I tell you."

I was enjoying being able to give orders, especially orders to Miss Nancy Clancy who usually gave orders to me. I enjoyed the way Basil turned so seriously to his drones and passed my commands on to them.

First I had Apis and Romeo push the lever twice. That gave us a good space in which to start the letter. I climbed up the keys and pointed to the one marked M. "Jump on this one, Basil!" I called, and Basil and all his friends piled on to the M key.

"When do I do something?" Miss Nancy Clancy called.

"When we get to the ends of words!" I told her. "Give us a chance."

She tossed her head, folded her arms and sat across the space bar. Basil's drones weighed the key down and suddenly there was a clear M on the paper. "Hooray!" called Apis and Romeo at the same time. It was the first time they'd ever agreed about anything. I jumped up one layer of keys to the J, hopped from H to G to F and then up to R. "This one!" I told Basil. Basil and his drones ran up, tumbled on top of each other and pressed the R. "Now!" I called to Nancy Clancy.

And so it went. After an hour's work we had a letter that read:

mr and mrs kelly
the hillside
northtown
australia.

dear mother and farther,

im quiet well and staying with friends my sides better now so dont worry and will see you soon

yore loving sun

ned.

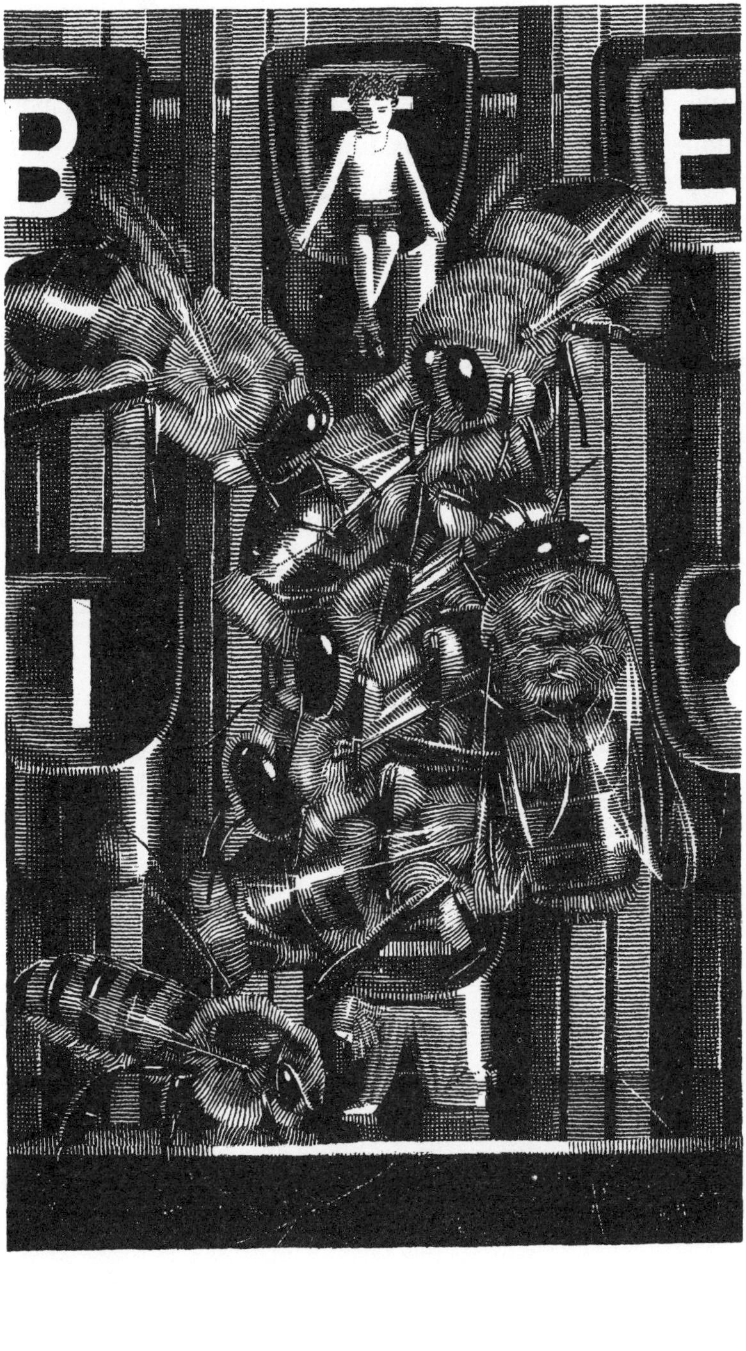

I looked at the others when the letter was finished. Nancy Clancy was riding the space bar as if it were a rocking horse. Romeo and Apis looked at me quietly, and the drones were tired but happy, along the bottom row of keys. I felt shy because of all the work they'd done for me. "Thank you, thank you all," I said.

"Now," said Apis, "we only have to take it to your parents' house."

"Oh no," I said. "Miss Such will take it. When she gets home and sees it there. We couldn't have a better postman."

"Postwoman," said Nancy Clancy, jolting on the space bar.

I found myself crying again. "What's the matter *now*?" she asked.

I shook my head. "It's just good to have such good friends."

"Well, silly," she said. "Who doesn't know that?"

There was the sound of thunder in the mountains and the bees all turned their heads to it.

"I think we should go home," said Apis.

Basil seemed less happy now, as if the thunder had reminded him of unpleasant things. "Don't forget," he told us. "You promised to talk to the Queen."

10

Ned Kelly Squashed

AND SO, THE next morning, when Queen Selma went past after breakfast, we were waiting for her. Again Apis moved in amongst the fanners and fussers and dragged some of them away by their hind legs. Again Apis spoke to the Queen. But this time Selma did not have as far to travel to speak to us. We were crouched on the wall of wax just above her head.

"I see you have got used to climbing," she said to us.

I hung by one hand to show just how good I *had* got at it. Miss Nancy Clancy did the same. But before we could speak to Queen Selma, Romeo pushed past us, bowed his head and began to talk.

"Madam, you see before you a humble drone," he squawked. "Yet my only wish in life is to be your attendant, your servant, your knight, your champion..."

"Is he joking?" Selma asked Apis.

"No," said Apis. "No, he means it."

"You want to be my knight?" asked Selma, giggling a little. But when she saw Romeo's hurt face, she stopped.

"I can tell good jokes too," said Romeo in a tiny voice.

"Oh?" said Selma. "Oh, I like good jokes. Give me a for-instance joke."

"All right." Romeo thought hard. "Why did the man stand behind the mule?"

"I don't know. Why?"

"He thought he'd get a kick out of it."

Queen Selma tossed her head with laughter and Romeo rushed to tell her another joke.

"What happened to the man who swallowed his spoon?"

"Do tell, Sir Romeo."

"He couldn't stir."

Selma laughed again in her scratchy way.

At my side Apis whispered, "Her voice is going. Notice that? Poor Selma."

But Romeo, listening to the Queen's chuckles, was twitching with joy.

"All right," said Selma in the end. "You have a job, Mr Romeo, or should I say *Sir* Romeo. You can be my joker. My joking knight. Do you think you can manage it?"

"Oh," squeaked Romeo. "Oh..."

"A half dozen jokes a day. At the very least. What do you say?"

"Oh...Oh..."

"He hasn't said anything yet," Nancy Clancy muttered a little cruelly.

"Oh you won't regret it, Your Majesty. You'll laugh all your days."

"He'll go and listen to Tony Brain's Funny Hour," whispered Apis. I had listened to the Funny Hour when I was a little younger. Amongst children in my class it was said to be babyish. But a lot of us listened to it secretly.

"They have dozens of jokes on that," Apis went on. "Then back he'll come and tell them all to Selma."

Meanwhile, Romeo was trying to bow and falling over instead.

"Join me then," Selma told him. She shoo-ed the fanners and escorts away and let Romeo stand beside her. Together, she and the plump drone were about to walk away across the honeycomb. It was then that I remembered my promise to Basil.

"Queen Selma," I said. She didn't hear me at first and I began to blush. "Your Majesty." It came out squeaky, as if I were Romeo.

Selma nudged Romeo to be quiet and looked at me with her head to one side.

"I promised my friend Basil..."

"*Basil?* Basil is your friend?"

"Well, he very kindly helped me," I muttered. "He helped me send a message to my mother and father. And he wanted to know if—as a pay-back—I'd ask you something. And it's this. He wants me to ask you not to kick the drones out of the hive when the autumn rains come." I got the message out, trying not to blush more and not to let her confuse me.

She was very still. Her eyes were like black diamonds, and I couldn't tell what she was thinking. After a long time she spoke. "Who told you I bothered to throw drones out of the hive?" Her voice was icy. "Autumn rains or not?"

"Well, I don't mean..." I said in a hurry. "Well, Bas—I don't know."

"You are a visitor here, young Kelly. Why do you think you can ask me stupid questions about drones? About what I intend to do in the autumn? Drones! There'll always be drones and you're not to discuss them, do you understand?"

"But Basil was so—"

"*Do you understand, Master Kelly?*"

In those days everyone called boys Master This or That when they were trying to shut them up or frighten them. I looked up at the immense eyes of Queen Selma. I felt both properly shut up and fully frightened. If the whole school staff, Headmaster and all the teachers, had called me out of class and accused me of bank robbery, I couldn't have felt worse.

"Yes," I muttered and lowered my eyes. I've failed Basil, I thought.

Selma must then have turned to Apis, for I heard her say, "If you can't teach your visitors manners, then there will simply have to be no more visitors."

By the time I looked up again, Selma and Romeo and all the courtier bees had left.

"Well, you nearly got me into deep trouble," said Nancy Clancy. "It's all right for you—if you're turned out you can just go back home. But if I'm sent away, where do I go?"

"Why didn't you help me ask her?" I wanted to know.

"I knew it wouldn't be any use," she said. "I knew she'd say what she said. I knew it."

"Besides, besides," Apis murmured, "it isn't exactly like Basil said. And you got your message away. That was the important part."

Miss Nancy Clancy began singing in an annoying way: "If you're just a human bean, you can't ask questions of a Queen."

I didn't even bother to groan.

11

Wasp War

LITTLE LATER, Apis flew out of the hive. I was beginning to feel better about my talk with Selma. So Miss Clancy and I sat inside the doorway of the cave at the place where Basil and the drones usually met. We watched the workers fly in and out and the guards, in a straight line, doing their duty at the door. We could see, out of the doorway, the blue sky, and the green leaves of the mountain ash in which we all lived.

Miss Nancy Clancy suddenly spoke. "What do you think of that stupid Miss Such?"

"What's stupid about Miss Such?"

"Not wanting to marry that nice Doctor Morgan."

"I think," I began, "I think that's very sensible of Miss Such. If you listen to most people you begin to think all anyone ever wanted was to get married. And if a girl can marry a doctor—most people think that's like winning the lottery."

"Marrying Doctor Morgan is like winning something," said Miss Nancy Clancy in a daze. I could see that Doctor Morgan had got into Miss Nancy Clancy's heart and brain, and I was jealous, I don't know why.

"I think marriage is boring," I said. "Look at Mrs Abey. You can have terrible children. Maybe if Miss Such married Doctor Morgan they'd have a child as terrible as Maurie Abey. And that'd be boring. Trying to get Maurie to behave like a human. No, you wouldn't want to marry Doctor Morgan."

"Perhaps," said Miss Clancy squinting at me, "I know more about what I want than you do."

It was hard to think of what to say next, and while I *was* thinking I saw Nancy Clancy look up to the doorway. In an instant, her face turned to a sick white and a look of terror widened her eyes. I dragged my own head round towards the entrance to the hive and saw a face I will remember until I die. It was a skull-shaped face of black and yellow, the eyes were black and cold and cruel, and above the eyes were black stiff feelers. Between this face and us lay a twitching and dying young guard bee.

"Wasps!" Nancy Clancy managed to hiss. "It's wasps!"

The wasp that had just stung the young guard now turned to fight off two other guards. I could see that there were at least five wasps fighting guard bees in the doorway where, when we began talking about Miss Such and Doctor Morgan, all had been peaceful. Bodies of the dead lay all over the entrance—the poisonous stings of the large raiders had killed them. But more bees were rushing from the inside of the hive to take the place of those the wasps had finished. I saw a young worker fling herself on the creature whose face had first frightened me, but the wasp easily threw her off, jumped on her and pushed into her body a great black sting.

"Stay still," Nancy Clancy managed to tell me. "Don't move. They've come after honey."

The terrible black and yellow monster took one more step towards us and I wanted to run. It wasn't much comfort to me to see that, closer to the door itself, dozens of guards were stinging one of the other wasps through its armor. It wasn't much comfort to hear it roar as the bee poison began to work on it.

It was then that Apis flew in with her load of pollen and nectar, straight in over the terrible battlefield, and jumped abroad the wasp closest to Nancy Clancy and myself. Apis lay there on the thing's back, going limp, and her weight and the weight of her load made it hard for the enemy to throw her off. She looked like a cowboy riding a bronco. I could see her own sting bared, but she could not put it into the wasp unless she stood up on its back, and if she stood up on its back, it would have bounced her off and finished her quickly.

At last two more workers joined Apis. One was hurled off and the wasp trod on it and stung it to death. Apis could do nothing but cling to the creature's back.

Closer to the door another raider fell under its weight of bees and was stung again and again. Now a crowd of workers turned to Apis's brute. One or two of them were trampled and run through, but most of them pushed *their* stings in through the wasp's yellow and black armor. After a second the creature's front legs gave way. I began to feel sorry for it then. I knew it wanted now only to fly out of the hive and never to see any honey again, if only they would let it go. But the bees gave it no mercy. Their

stings punched into its sides. The poor skull-faced wasp rolled on its side, roaring and choking as the bee poison began to reach its heart.

Suddenly every thing was still again. I looked around me and saw the floor of the cave-hive covered with dead bees and with the five giant bodies of the wasps. Young workers tugged these to the door of the hive and pushed them down over the edge. Next the workers who had died trying to keep the wasps out of the hive were carried away. No one made a speech, the way humans always seem to do after a battle. I think it was better not to make a speech.

Half of Apis's pollen had been knocked out of her baskets by the fight, but she limped away now, too tired to speak to us, to give in what was left.

"Does this happen every summer?" I asked Miss Clancy.

"Oh yes," she said, nodding her head. I could tell she was not lying, for she was still too frightened to lie. "Sometimes it's worse than this, sometimes dozens of them make a raid. It's terrible." She began crying. "Why do they do it? Why do the wasps come?"

"Don't cry like that," I said.

"All those brave bees," she went on, still shedding tears but looking at the workers dragging the bodies of dead bees to the door. "Whoever remembers them?"

"I'll always remember them," I said. And I suppose I always have.

That night, as I lay on the bed trying to get the picture of the wasp's face out of my mind, I could hear Miss Nancy Clancy whimpering in her sleep like a puppy. "It's all right," I would whisper at her, and even in her sleep she seemed to hear me.

I thought, in the morning I'll go back home. But I knew that I was lying to myself. I liked Apis too much to leave yet, and I suppose I even liked Miss Nancy Clancy. And in the morning the day was bright, and we flew out with Apis and played on the boughs of a box brush and heard serials at Mrs Maguire's, because Mrs Maguire didn't have a waspy son like Maurie Abey. And we saw Selma go by our door with Romeo still asking her riddles.

"What is black and white and red all over?"

"Tell me, Sir Romeo."

"A blushing zebra."

"Hah! Tell me another."

"What time is it if an elephant sits on your beehive?"

"I don't know, I don't know."

"Time to get a new hive."

And hearing him tell his awful jokes in his squeaky voice, we felt normal again.

12

A New Queen

It began to rain. Bees don't like the rain, it makes them unhappy. No one can go out gathering food, for the valley's fat raindrops would knock a bee off its course and blind it and daze it. So Apis had nothing to do and couldn't even get up to Mrs Maguire's to hear the radio serials.

"You are, poor bee," Miss Clancy told her, "a study in brown, when the radio's off and the rain comes down."

The wind beat against our mountain ash, we could hear the branches waving and thrashing. The escorts gathered around Selma to keep her warm, more and more of the bees went into huddles, close to each other, trying to keep cozy. The only work that went on was the feeding of the young bees and of the babies in their cells, and the guarding of the door. Sometimes the wind would creep round the doorway and blow a guard bee over and over. It was a dull time and even Miss Clancy and I felt blue.

It rained for three days, and just as it stopped, Selma roused herself and went for a tour of the hive with all her courtiers. Near our apartment, she met Apis.

I was surprised by what Apis said to her.

"Do you think," Apis asked her, "that it might be time for you to move out and find a new hive?"

Selma raised her head in her queenly way. "Whatever for? Because of all that rain?"

"Not, not because of the rain." Apis shuffled on her feet and looked uneasy. "But there may be other reasons why you and some of us should move out."

Selma replied grandly, "There is no reason I know of on earth why I should leave my hive. Do you know of one?"

Apis seemed to shrug, if a bee can shrug.

"I don't see the point of this kind of talk at all," said Selma, moving away.

Apis grunted a little and, turning, saw us. Our eyes must have been full of questions.

"Can you keep a secret?" she asked us.

We nodded over and over. Children have always been like that—they itch all over when a secret is mentioned, and they don't stop itching until they know what the secret is.

"I thought," Apis murmured, "that Selma might want to move away and start a new hive, because the new Queen is about to be born."

"Why is that a secret?" I asked the bee.

"Because Selma would be jealous if she knew."

"But Selma laid the egg in the first place."

"That wouldn't stop her being jealous."

We followed Apis down the honeycomb—we were now so used to climbing—and reached the part of the hive where the Queen Bee cells hung. They were bigger than ordinary cells, and there were many of them. Around them, a crowd of workers had got together and were watching, not buzzing, not moving a feeler or a wing.

"How do they know she's going to be born today?" I whispered.

"They can tell, that's all," Apis hissed back. "This is the seventeenth day you know. The seventeenth day since the first egg was laid."

Somewhere, in another part of the hive, Selma wandered glumly in the midst of a crowd of bees listening to Romeo's supply of jokes. Because he hadn't been out to Mrs Maguire's to hear the Funny Hour, he must have been running short of riddles.

Here though, where Nancy Clancy and Apis and I were, no one was bored, no one needed to speak.

At last the bottom of the cell began to split open, and we could see the new Queen's head. She bit away more and more of the cell until at last she was able to drag her whole body through and stand hanging from the outside of the cell. She was a beautiful new Queen. As she stood on the honeycomb, she looked at us. She shone, she was dazzling, not weak and complaining like a human baby, but fully grown and strong. As soon as the workers and drones who were all around her saw her shining black eyes, they crowded against her, waving their feelers, fluttering their wings. I expected them to break out cheering, forgetting that none of them but Apis and Basil knew how to cheer. But watching them, we knew that there was a new Queen in the hive. What would happen to the old Queen?

"What will happen to Selma?" I asked Apis.

But before Apis could tell me, a second young Queen began to struggle out of her cell. Before she could get properly on her feet, her sister the new Queen rushed to her and pushed her sting into her many times over. The sight made me sick. In my shock, I cried, "Why did she do that?"

"Shush!" Nancy Clancy told me.

But Apis explained. "There can only be one Queen," she said softly. "She has to sting all her sisters as they're born."

I was still trying not to be sick. That was it—I couldn't stay on in a hive where sisters killed each other.

"Take me home!" I told Apis.

"Shush!" Nancy Clancy said again.

I climbed away from that terrible place, back up the honeycomb wall. I wanted to be on my own. But Apis followed me. "Ned," she called. I stopped climbing. "Are you shocked? Is that it? Are you shocked because the new Queen kills her sisters?"

"Yes," I said in a small voice.

"She has to do it. There can only be one Queen in a hive."

"But it's awful," I said.

"Wasn't there a human Queen once, called Elizabeth? And didn't she kill her cousin Mary who also wanted to be Queen? Didn't she cut Mary's head off?"

"That was in the old days. That was different. And it was wrong. It was wrong even then."

"Was it, Ned? The world is full of sad things that can't be changed."

"Then will she sting Selma?" I didn't want anything to happen to Selma, I'd got used to her squawky laugh and her crazy royal ways.

Before Apis could answer me, I heard a flurry of noise below us. Looking down, I saw that Selma had arrived on the scene. Someone must have told her what was happening, that a new Queen had been born. I saw her look at her cruel young daughter. Both Queens stood very still and straight. They walked towards each other and lightly touched with their feelers and then stood and stared at each other. They did not make a sound or try to sting, and all the bees in the hive seemed to be watching as they silently faced one another. Then Selma turned and walked away. Everyone began buzzing now.

Apis said, "You like Selma. Well, Selma hatched once, years ago, and had to kill all *her* sisters. Because that's how Queens have always been."

"What will happen now?"

"Selma will leave. And some of us will leave with her. Remember what I told you in the past. I said, in seventeen days a new Queen will be born. And then everything will be turned upside down."

I had to admit that. Things *had* been turned upside down.

13

Moving and Maurie Abey

THAT EVENING WE sat in our favorite place near the mouth of the cave, looking at the sun falling bright red behind the mountains. There were Apis, Romeo, Basil and, of course, Miss Nancy Clancy and I.

"Well, I'm going with Selma," Basil said. "The boys and I don't trust her much, but that new Queen really looks like a tough one."

"And of course I'm going with Selma too," Romeo said. "Most drones won't. All most of them can say is how beautiful the new Queen is. They'll stay here and fly in her wedding flight..."

"And when the autumn rains come," said Basil, "she'll boot them out, that one. You can bet on that. Oh yes."

I didn't know what they were talking about...drones...wedding flights. Apis saw me frowning and laughed. "I think our young friend Ned doesn't quite know what's happening. As I told you, when a new Queen is born, the old Queen moves out and looks for a new place to build her hive. She takes with her, as

I said, any of the workers who want to go and even some of the drones—"

"*Even* of the drones?" asked Basil with some anger.

"—even of the drones who want to go with her. Most of the drones will stay on though, because in a little while the new Queen will fly out on her wedding flight and the drones will follow. She will fly high until there's only one drone left near her."

"And that one drone will be allowed to join with her," Basil explained, "and put his seed in her body so that she will be able to lay eggs from which bees will be born. There'll only be one lucky drone, all the rest will just fly in circles. But I have to admit it, most of the lads are so thick that each one of them thinks he'll be the one who'll mate with the Queen. Idiots!"

"Are you coming with us, Ned?" Apis asked me. "Or do you prefer the new Queen too?"

I couldn't imagine a bee hive without Apis and Nancy Clancy. "If you're going, I want to go."

"Oh I'm going with Selma all right," said Apis. "This new one looks too vain to want to learn radio. This young one will work us into the ground." She sighed. "Besides, I like old Selma."

"And as for old Miss Nancy Clancy," said Miss Nancy Clancy, "I'll follow Apis, that's my fancy."

All at once I felt very happy. We were leaving the hive where the wasps had fought, where the savage young Queen had murdered her sisters. We would go to a new bright place that had no terrible memories.

"Yes, yes," I said. "I'm going too." But no one seemed to be sure just when the move would happen.

"Nancy Clancy," said Apis, "should have her books and cups

and candles ready to go at a moment's notice." Apis would make sure there were two strong young workers detailed to carry Miss Clancy's furniture—her table, chair and bed—on their backs.

"One thing is certain," Basil told us. "If Selma doesn't go soon, the new Queen will turn on her and drive her out at the point of a sting."

Overnight, Apis and the other workers who had decided to travel with Queen Selma got ready for the journey. They were allowed to go to the cells where honey was stored and suck it up into their bodies. They fetched Selma and took her for a training run over the surface of the honeycomb, trying to get some of her fat off so that she could fly better and further.

"Why, why?" asked Selma, puffing along. "Why run me around like this?"

"You don't have to be told," Apis answered.

Romeo ran behind the others, hardly keeping up, no breath left for telling riddles.

"Can't I," asked Selma, "since I'm a royal being, have some of that delicious jelly?" Apis refused in her toughest, huskiest voice, and all the other workers buzzed in a way that meant *no!*

"Oh-h-h!" said Selma. "Moving is hell."

Miss Nancy Clancy and I were woken before the sun had risen. Apis and two strong young workers had come to collect Miss Clancy's furniture. We tied the bed to the back of one of the workers, using a length of Nancy Clancy's old, old rope. We slipped her cups, *The Butterfly Ball and the Grasshopper's Feast* and her other books beneath the mattress. On the back of the second worker we loaded the table, chair and bucket.

As the bees left with her furniture, Miss Nancy Clancy looked around her empty cell. I once saw a lady called Mrs Rudge, a farmer's wife, look around her kitchen like that the morning the Rudges sold their farm and moved away.

"Come on," I said, taking her by the elbow and urging her out of the door.

In the doorway of the hive hundreds of bees were gathered, most of them full of honey. Selma stood, much thinner than I'd ever seen her, amongst a little knot of servants and fanners. She looked miserable and Romeo was trying to make her laugh.

"If a carrot and a cabbage," Romeo was squeaking, "if a carrot and a cabbage ran a race, which would win?"

"Who knows?" asked Selma mournfully. "Who cares?"

"The cabbage wins. Because it's a head."

"I see," said Selma, not laughing.

"Well," Romeo gasped, "why is it wrong to whisper?"

"I suppose you'll insist on telling me the answer," Selma groaned.

"Because it is not aloud."

Selma went on groaning. The sun rose, but there was thunder in the hills. Apis told us. "It always thunders when a Queen leaves her hive. An old bee told me. It always thunders."

"Why are we waiting," asked Nancy Clancy, "here, all still,
When we should be flying over the hill
Searching for a hole in a hollow old tree,
A palace for Selma and a cell for me...?"

Saying this rhyme, Nancy Clancy sounded worried, as if she was not just making verse to annoy her friends.

"Soon, soon," Apis told her. "Soon the scout bees will be back."

I knew that we wouldn't move straight to a new hive. First we would all swarm. The scout bees would find a branch or some other place where all the bees could cluster together and wait. While all Selma's bees hung there in a great bunch, the scouts—who were the older, wiser and stronger bees—would search for a place to build a hive. The search might take a few hours, or a few days, and meantime Nancy Clancy and I, as well as Apis, Basil and Romeo, would have to hang in a bunch of bees from some tree branch.

It was only a little while before the scout bees landed in the doorway. They began dancing, raising their tails and pointing to the place they had found for us to swarm on. "On my back!" Apis ordered suddenly. We had only just obeyed her when all the bees around us took off, Apis with them. We shot out of the mouth of the hive like water from a hose, all flying together, all going in the same direction. I hung on to Apis with one hand and raised my other arm the way a cowboy riding a wild horse does. "Weeh-hee!" I yelled, and Miss Nancy Clancy laughed, and everyone seemed much happier now that they no longer had to shuffle round the doorway of the old hive thinking, "We'll never see this place again."

We flew for a mile down river, all very close together. I could have reached out with my hands or feet and touched the flapping wings of the bees on either side of Apis or the ones below her. I could see, in the openings between the brown bodies of the crowd of bees, Mrs Abey's place on the side of the hill. But I did not notice that Maurie, sent home from school again for being Maurie, was watching from the Abeys' back fence. I did not know that seeing us swarm by he ran and got a milk bucket and its lid and began to follow us.

At last the leaders landed on a branch of a spotted gum near the cow paddocks of a farmer called Mr Morrison. They clung to the branch with their spiky feet, and the ones who landed next clung to the backs of the ones who had landed first, and so it went on, till by the time Apis, Miss Clancy and I arrived at the swarming place, a great ball of bees was hanging from the branch. Somewhere in the middle of it was Selma and her joker, Romeo, who was still probably muttering riddles at his Queen. We landed on the outside of the mass of bees and hung on. Nancy Clancy and I in our turn clung to Apis's wide back. The scout bees were already flying away, looking at last for a proper place for a hive.

"What if they don't find a place?" I asked Apis.

"Don't talk nonsense," Apis snapped at me. "They always do."

"I've heard from bees in the past," said Nancy Clancy, "that if it rains hard, or if no one can agree on where we should live, then we just stay here until we drop off, one by one."

"I won't tolerate that talk!" Apis told her.

"What do we do now then?" asked Miss Clancy.

"I suggest we have a sleep."

And before long we were all dozing in the early morning sun.

But Miss Nancy Clancy had not mentioned another of the fates that often overtakes swarms of wild bees. Bee farmers capture them, lock them into a hive or a bucket and take them home with them. And that was what Maurie Abey knew. He had run behind us so that he could catch Selma and all her bees with his bucket, and then he would sell us all to some farmer, perhaps to Mr Morrison himself. Even while we dozed on Apis's back, on the outside of the swarm, Maurie was searching amongst the trees to find where we had landed. At last he saw us and came tramping through the tree and over the muddy grass towards us. We were above his head, so he found a solid stick, held it in one hand and, with the other, put the bucket right under the place where we were hanging. He intended to use the stick to knock us off the branch and into the bucket. Then before anyone could bite him, he would put the lid on the bucket and set out to sell us.

The first I knew of it was when Apis began jigging up and down. She was dancing a warning to the others. I woke up, looked below me and saw the giant grinning face of horrible Maurie, his giant gleaming eyes, his dirty hair, a giant smear of jam on his chin from his messy lunch. As I watched, he raised his stick and tried to sweep the whole bunch of us into his pail.

But it didn't all happen the way he wanted it to. The bees did not land in his bucket. Instead, disturbed on their branch by the dancing of Apis, they saw Maurie and decided he was a more comfortable place to swarm. In two seconds Maurie was covered from the top of his greasy hair to the laces of his shoes with Selma's bees. Even Apis, carrying Nancy Clancy and me, landed on his head.

I knew exactly what Maurie Abey himself knew—that if he moved much, he would be stung hundreds of times. Even if I didn't like him, I didn't want him to be filled with all that bee poison. I noticed that he was now doing the first wise thing he had ever done in his life. He was keeping very still but I could hear him whimpering through his open mouth.

"Oh no," he was sobbing. "Oh no!"

"Come on," I said to Miss Nancy Clancy. I had climbed off Apis's back.

"Where are you going?" asked Apis.

"I'm going to talk to him."

"That brute?" said Miss Nancy Clancy.

"Yes. You come too."

"Why should I?" she asked. But she began to climb down with me, making for Maurie's bee-encrusted ear. We climbed over the backs of hundreds of bees, but they didn't seem to mind. At last we were facing the shadowy hole through which Maurie heard things.

"Maurie!" I yelled. "Don't move. They'll go away in the end. So please, keep still."

"If you want a big surprise," yelled Nancy Clancy, not nearly so helpfully, "Yell and wriggle and blink your eyes."

Maurie began to twitch. At any second he might start running. But the bees would stay with him and, angered, put their stings in.

"Maurie," I called again, "listen Maurie, please don't move."

Once again Nancy Clancy was no help. "If you'd like to be one big sting," she shouted, "Blow your nose like anything."

"Nancy!" I barked. Maurie twitched again. "No, no, keep still please, Maurie. Do you know who I am? I'm Ned Kelly, the boy you tried to run over with a bike, that's who I am. But if you keep still and don't move, you'll live to go home to your mother, and by tomorrow you'll be running someone else over."

"Oh, oh," he kept saying, as if he would never run anyone else over ever.

"Miss Clancy," I said, "don't say anything to upset him."

I climbed back up Maurie's head, or rather I climbed back up the backs of the bees who coated Maurie all over. Apis was waiting for me. "If you did a dance," I asked her, "could you get all these bees to leave Maurie?"

But Apis could not hear me, because so many bees were buzzing and Maurie was loudly moaning.

"Can you get the others to leave Maurie and go back to the tree?" I yelled.

"I could do a dance," said Apis, "but why should I do a dance to save that monster from being stung?"

I reminded her that whoever stung Maurie would not be able to get their stings out again. Was Maurie worth the trouble, I asked her.

"All right," said Apis. "You behave as if he were your brother or something."

She began to dance over the backs of her own brothers and sisters. The dance said, "Let's leave this miserable lump and go back to the tree." In twos and threes and then in bigger groups they began to do that, leaving the surface of Maurie's clothes and body and swarming again on the branch.

We climbed on Apis's back. Now nearly every bee had left Maurie but he still stood whimpering, his bucket in his hand.

"He tried to catch the bees," said Nancy Clancy. "But the bees caught him."

"You can go now, Maurie," I called. As Apis and Nancy Clancy and I rose to rejoin the swarm Maurie dropped his bucket. It fell on the ground with a thud and a clank. He began running.

I found out long after that Maurie ran straight to school and told Miss Such that he had been covered all over with bees, and while he stood there frightened, tiny voices had told him to be still. And that he knew while he stood there so terrified, coated all over with bees, what it was like to suffer and not be able to move or answer back. So now, he told Miss Such, he was never going to be cruel to smaller children again.

Of course, in real life people don't often change completely. But although Maurie still picked on smaller children and dumb animals, he was never again so out-and-out savage as he had been in the past. So that he did learn a little something from his meeting with Selma's bees.

14

The Hive at Major Steel's

"They're back," Apis said, waking me. I'd slept all night on her, leaning against Miss Nancy Clancy, and although it had been a strange way to spend the night, I had slept well.

"Who?" I asked her, holding on with one hand and stretching with the other. "Who's back?"

"The scouts. The scouts are all back."

Looking down, we could see them dancing on the great ball of bees of which we ourselves were part.

"Some dance one way," I noticed. "Some dance another."

Apis said, "One of the scouts wants us to go inland. Another wants us to go across the river. Another wants us to go up the river and another still down. They've all found good places for a hive, or so they say. It depends on who wins the argument."

One of the scouts, the one who always waggled her tail in a down-river direction, danced up towards us. We could hear, in the way she pounded her feet, how much she wanted us to go her way. She must have found the right kind of hole for a hive and she was dancing her small heart out trying to convince all of us.

"She's waggling her tail faster than the others," said Miss Nancy Clancy. "I know that means something."

Apis nodded. "That means the place she found is closer than the holes the others found. I hope we go with her. I don't want to have to fly too far away from Mrs Maguire's radio."

In the middle of the cluster we could hear Romeo squeaking at the Queen. "The one who says *down-river* seems to have found a nice place," he told her.

The little dancer kept on dancing out her argument until I thought she'd fall over, tired out. But at last the other scouts began to dance like her. They had decided—like the rest of us—that she must have found the best place of all for a hive, and they too wanted to follow her.

She could tell now that everyone was on her side, and so she flew into the air, and the whole thick swarm followed her. We hadn't flown far, dodging amongst the trees, when I saw ahead of us an old house I'd visited once before. Once, a hundred years ago, it had been a fine two-story house of stone and plaster. It had been built by a man called Major Steel. Now no one lived there. That was for many reasons. Sometimes floods came into the ground floor, and even if anyone wanted to buy it, there were very few people in our valley who could have afforded to furnish it and do it up. Of course, all the children of the town called it a haunted house, because Major Steel had been so unhappy in it that he'd hanged himself. The story was that his wife had run away back to England and taken his son and daughter with her, and so poor

Major Steel had been all alone in his stone house in the bush and had been too lonely to live on. People told stories of seeing Major Steel's ghost on dark nights; fishermen coming home from the river said they'd seen him, and so did some of the big boys from the high school who had gone out one night to hunt rabbits. Well, you can't always believe fishermen or big boys. Just the same, as I neared the stone house that morning on Apis's back, I held my breath and wondered about poor Major Steel.

High up on one of the walls of the house was a small hole where the scout had landed and was dancing joyously. Then she stood still and pushed bees through the hole as if she was saying, "[You] have a look at the place and you'll see it's exactly right."

Apis and Nancy and I at last got inside the hole in the wall.

"Oh," said Apis, "this is good. Oh this is grand!"

All the other bees were buzzing madly, as pleased as Apis was. I could see even the workers who still had Nancy Clancy's furniture on their backs were jumping with excitement.

Major Steel had been a rich man in the early days of our town and his house had been built with two walls, an outside one of stone and an inside one of bricks. As you can see from the drawing, the hole the scout had found led through into the space between the walls and above us was a beam of wood from which the honeycomb could be hung. Even I could tell it was a wonderful place for a hive. I noticed as well that across from the main opening was a small hole in the brick wall. From it, we would be able to see into the inside of the house.

I pointed to this place, laughed and said to Miss Nancy Clancy, "We can sit there and look out for the ghost."

"Ghost?"

"Major Steel's ghost. He used to live here."

"Oh, oh," she said and frowned. "My father knew a Major Steel."

I shivered when she said this. It was so hard to remember that Nancy Clancy was a hundred and twenty years old.

Guards had already taken up their position at the door. They stood in a straight line, facing outwards towards the world from which wasps and Maurie Abeys and other dangers might come. Selma stood on the doorway's inside edge and seemed to shake herself. Straight-away, workers flew up to the wooden beam above our heads and hung from it in a long, straight line. Apis joined them, after first unloading Nancy Clancy and me on to the floor.

Nancy and I watched the bees working high above us, watched them clinging to the roof and to each other. Taking little plates of wax from their stomachs, cutting them into shape with their mouths, sticking them to the roof, molding them into rows of beautiful six-sided cells, honeycomb and cells for pollen and for egg laying, and one of them an apartment for Nancy Clancy and me.

Selma's group—Romeo, the bees whose job it was to keep her cool or warm or happy—came and waited near Nancy Clancy and me while the work went ahead far above us. "Oh they're good workers," we heard Selma keep saying. "They're good girls."

By mid-day the good girls had built a great comb with thousands of cells, and already some of them were flying out to get nectar and pollen to pack into the hive.

"Tomorrow, I suppose," Selma told us dreamily. "I'll start laying. Not Queen eggs, no sir. I don't want any more uppity young queens. But workers, that's what we need. A lot more workers."

Nancy Clancy and I spent that day telling stories, some of them true. She told me, for instance, about the convicts who used to come from England by ship to Port Macquarie, wearing chains on their legs all the way. She told me about princesses she'd met, though I didn't quite believe her. I told about trouble I'd got into at school, and most of that wasn't true either. I made myself sound like Maurie Abey, whereas I was really easily scared by teachers.

We played charades and *I Spy*.

"I spy with my little eye something beginning with S.R."

"S.R.?"

"Yes. S.R."

I looked around. I couldn't see anything in the new hive that began with S.R.

"Sandy Rock?" I guessed.

"No. Give up?"

"All right."

"Stupid Romeo!" shouted Nancy Clancy in triumph.

"That's not a proper *I Spy*."

"Yes it is. It's a perfectly proper *I Spy*. It's as perfectly proper as N.K.D."

"N.K.D.?"

"Ned Kelly the Dunce," she said.

I would pretend to be angry. But I enjoyed the games and the arguments.

15

Duffers

WHEN APIS WENT off alone on a pollen or nectar trip she would often leave us in the hole that opened into the inside of the house. From this point we could see the living room of the house, and its dusty old fireplace. Sometimes we would try to imagine what it must have been like when there were books and toys, armchairs and pictures and children in that old room. But mainly we played our games.

We were sitting there late one afternoon, playing one of our usual guessing games, when the front door of the house opened and two men came in. I know that it always happens in stories like this that children are hiding in a haunted house when in come two villains. It happens in *Tom Sawyer,* for example.

But these two men weren't villains. In fact one was Mr Horne, father of my friends, Jack and Kate Horne, the ones who had been with me that day I'd got sick and gone to the hospital. The other man was Maurie Abey's father, Clarence Abey by name. They both sat down on the living room floor and began rolling cigarettes. It was only when they'd finished this little job that they began talking.

"Well," said Mr Horne, his voice booming in the big empty room, "I know it happens a lot. Duffing. Half the people wouldn't ever eat meat if they didn't duff a few cattle."

"That's right," said Clarence Abey, "that's the bare truth."

"Duffing? What's duffing?" Nancy Clancy asked me.

"Stealing. Stealing cattle," I told her.

Mr Horne went on. "But I never thought I'd want to steal a prize bull like that, a big expensive bull."

"Well, it's going to be easy," Clarence Abey told him. "We get him out of Morrison's paddock about three o'clock tomorrow morning. Then my mate Trevor comes along with his truck and we load the bull on to the back and take him over the mountains, to one of those good western towns, and we sell him. And won't he just sell, Jimmy. He's such a beauty. Those western farmers—the wealthy ones anyway—will be lining up to buy him."

Mr Horne made a doubtful noise with his teeth.

"Aren't you sick of never having any money though?" Clarence Abey asked him. "Aren't you sick of seeing your missus in the same sad old dresses?"

"I'm sick," said Mr Horne, "of sending my daughter to school in a dress made out of old flour bags."

Clarence Abey nodded. "Then help me duff this bull. Come on. They tell me you can really handle bulls, talk to them, soothe them down. Help me duff the bull, eh?"

After a long think, Mr Horne nodded. "What's the bull's name?"

"Oh, he's got some fancy stud name but Morrison just calls him Fred."

"All right, all right."

"Have you got an alarm clock?"

"I don't sleep much," said Mr Horne. It sounded very flat the way he said it, as if he got no fun out of life at all. "I'll be awake at three o'clock in the morning."

And so they agreed to meet and duff the bull. Clarence Abey went, but Jimmy Horne sat on, finishing his thin cigarette. I should have felt sorry for Mr Morrison, the farmer who might soon lose his prize bull, but I felt sorry for Mr Horne instead and even for Clarence Abey. They'd looked as lost and unhappy as children and I never knew then that adults could be like that.

At last Mr Horne got up, stretched and left.

"I suppose," Miss Nancy Clancy said after a long silence, "you're going to rush to Miss Such's place and write a letter to Mr Morrison on the kindwriter?"

"The typewriter," I corrected her.

"Well, are you? Are you going to write a letter to Mr Morrison saying,

Dear Sir, your bull is going to be stolen,
I overheard it semi-colon,
Yours sincerely, a friend?"

In the cowboys films and in *Rick the Frontier Scout*, men who stole cattle were always mean and cruel, gun-toters who would shoot you down if you had anything they wanted. But Abey and

Horne were two frightened men, two men I knew, two men with wives and children and butchers' bills to pay.

"Well, well?" Nancy Clancy was asking.

"I can't send any messages," I told her. "Anyhow it isn't my business. Cattle duffing—it happens all the time in this valley. Every day nearly. The police don't even think it's any sort of crime, they're so used to it."

"Is that so?" she asked doubtfully.

"Yes. It is."

"A lot of those convicts," she told me, "the men who came to Port Macquarie in chains so long ago, a lot of them had been cattle stealers."

"Well, well," I said, "things are different these days."

And I wouldn't say anything more.

16

Arrest

THAT EVENING WE slept on Miss Nancy Clancy's bed in one of the clean new cells and, before the sun rose the next morning, were woken up by a loud animal noise. It sounded just like the moaning of a bull. We were soon to find out, it *was* the moaning of a bull. Some of the bees were already working, in fact they'd gone on working all night, but they did not seem to hear or be upset by the bull noise.

Nancy Clancy and I climbed out of our cell and took up our positions at the hole where, the day before, we had looked down on Mr Abey and Mr Horne. Now we saw them again. Mr Horne came in first, holding a lantern in one hand and dragging Fred the prize bull by a rope with the other. Behind Fred Mr Abey pushed, calling, "In there, Fred, in there." When they had Fred inside the old house, they tethered him to the ironwork around the old fire-place and then both sat down on the floor.

"All right," said Mr Horne, puffing, "where's your mate Trevor with the truck? Where is he, eh?"

"I don't know. It's no use asking me. Maybe he broke down."

"Maybe he got a bit of sense during the night," said Mr Horne, "and decided to stay in bed."

"He...he wouldn't do that to us." Mr Abey coughed. It was a bad, sick cough. "He'll come soon."

"That's no use," Mr Horne said. "We can't take Fred out into the open now. The sun's coming up."

In fact the first morning light was now coming in through the windows of the old house. Mr Abey sighed. "Oh," he said softly, "we're going to be stuck here all day with a bloody bull."

"Even if we tried to take Fred back," Mr Horne muttered, "old Morrison would see us. He gets up earlier than the sparrows."

"Hey, he's probably noticed already that Fred's gone. He's probably already rung the police."

"Oh hell!"

The two men hung their heads and shook them because of the trouble they were in. Fred bellowed loudly enough to be heard all over the valley.

"Shut up, Fred!" said Mr Abey.

Behind Nancy Clancy and me, the work of the bee hive had begun. Selma had already moved over the wax wall to begin laying eggs in the cells meant for egg laying. Apis was away on a morning flight. The bees were trying to make a lasting city for themselves here, in their hole in the wall, and they had no time for the human problems of Mr Horne and Mr Abey.

An hour passed, and Nancy Clancy and I watched the two men all the time. They talked about whether one of them ought to go and get some food from home while the other minded Fred. But then they decided not to. I imagined Kate and Jack Horne waking and asking where their father was. "Oh, he went off early," their mother would say. "He had some work or other to do." Then Kate would go and climb into her flour sack dress.

We did not leave that position all morning. We watched Fred moan and bellow and now and then drop some manure on the floor. We were still there, watching, at noonday. And Jimmy Horne and Clarence Abey were both dozing, their heads between their knees, when the police opened the front door of the house and walked in in their large black boots. I saw that the men in the police uniforms were Sergeant Kennedy and Constable Scanlon, and they were already in the room before the two cattle thieves were properly awake. Mr Morrison followed the police in.

"Fred," he said, pointing at the moaning bull. "That's old Fred."

Sergeant Kennedy told Mr Horne and Mr Abey to stand up. Jimmy Horne obeyed and leaned his head back until he was looking straight at our hole. There were tears on his cheeks.

"You won't believe me, Sergeant Kennedy," he said, "but we were just waiting for dark before we put the bull back."

"No, I don't believe you, Jimmy," the police sergeant said softly. "Well, maybe I do, but it doesn't make any difference."

There was silence while the sergeant wrote everyone's name and address down for when the case would come to court. "How much did you say your bull is worth, Mr Morrison?" he asked at last.

Mr Morrison named some great sum of money that made

both Nancy Clancy and me blink and stare at each other.

"Well, it's a very serious crime then," the sergeant muttered.

"Of course it's serious," Mr Morrison barked, caressing Fred's ears.

"For God's sake, Morrison," Jimmy Horne shouted. "It isn't as if we sold him or anything."

"You would've. In time."

"I've got a wife and two kids. If the judge puts me in Grafton jail..."

Morrison said, not very interested, "You should have thought about Grafton jail before you stole Fred."

"Both the men have families, Mr Morrison," Sergeant Kennedy said.

"All cattle duffers have families. That's why you police let them get away so easily. If I let them off, they'd be in the pub boasting about it, and every cattle thief in the valley would know he could get away with stealing Fred. No, charge them, Sergeant Kennedy."

So Kennedy put handcuffs on Clarence Abey and Jimmy Horne. Mr Horne stared at his wrists and shook the cuffs a little as if they might just melt away the way terrible situations melt away in dreams.

But Mr Horne's cuffs would not melt and the policeman led the two men out, and only Mr Morrison and the bull were left in the living room of the old house. The farmer looked over his shoulder and gave one angry shiver. I thought he might know we were watching him. Or perhaps he thought the unhappy ghost of Major Steel was in that very room. Anyhow he dragged Fred's rope and left as soon as he could, which wasn't very fast, since Fred got stuck in the door.

Nancy Clancy and I looked down at the empty room. I was feeling something I'd never known before—the desire to be amongst my own kind of people. Amongst humans. If Mr Horne was to go to Grafton jail, I wanted to be close to his daughter Kate and his son Jack, and I couldn't be close while I stayed in the hive.

I heard the noises of the hive behind me, and I knew it wasn't *my* sound.

"I think I might go home," I said.

"Oh?" said Nancy Clancy.

"Yes. That man who stole the bull. His kids are my best friends."

"Oh. Your *best* friends?"

"My best friends apart from you," I rushed to say.

"Oh...well. If you feel you ought to go back...then you should."

But I could see she wanted me to stay and couldn't make herself say it. I was pulled from one direction by Kate and Jack Horne, from the other by Miss Nancy Clancy. That was the first time anything like *that* had happened to me, too.

"Well," I said after a while. "I suppose I ought to stay here a bit longer. I'm having so much fun."

Miss Nancy Clancy smiled at me. "I spy with my little eye," she said, "something beginning with B.M."

"B.M.," I said, looking round the hive. "I give in."

"Bull's manure," she said with a broad grin.

17

Autumn Rains

AND SO I stayed on for the whole summer. Playing games with Nancy Clancy. Flying with Apis. Listening to Romeo's bad jokes. Watching the bees work indoors and out.

And I got very used to the hive. Even to the days when wasps came. Sometimes I didn't know until the wasp battle was over that it had even been going on at the main doorway of the hive. One day a trapdoor spider stumbled into the place and was stung and dragged away, and I saw nothing of it.

We thought the hot, hot summer would never end. No more villains came to Major Steel's house and although Miss Nancy Clancy and I sat up trembling one night, we never saw Major Steel's ghost. Our summer lives were spent half in the dark of the hive, half in the bright outdoors, and yet we never noticed that the summer was passing. The autumn rain that lashed Major Steel's house one morning told us *that* more clearly than anything. The golden summer is finished, said the rain.

When the long rains began Basil and his few friends came to the cell Nancy Clancy and I shared and clustered round our door. Their big drone eyes looked dull.

"It's started," said Basil.

"What?" I asked.

"We weren't given any honey this morning. We went up to the workers to be fed with honey as usual and weren't given a drop to eat." Nancy Clancy made a sad mouth, as if Basil's story wasn't a surprise to her. To take Basil's mind off his hunger, she began to read from one of her books. The noise of the rain forced her to read very loudly, and even the drones, who could not understand what she was saying, seemed to be comforted by her voice.

She was half way through *The Grasshopper's Feast* when Selma and her courtiers passed below us. We could see Romeo trying to keep up with them and squeaking, "What's the difference between a postage stamp and a woman?"

"I don't want to hear," Selma told him.

"Your Majesty, please try to guess..."

"What? What did you say? Are you trying to give *me* orders?"

"I was suggesting," said Romeo, "that you might try to guess what the difference is between a postage stamp and a woman?"

"*You* were suggesting? Does it at all seem likely to you that I mightn't be interested in what the difference is?"

"Ah...well..."

"I'm trying to say, Sir Romeo, our time together is over. It's all very well to listen to jokes in the summer, but the autumn rains are here, and the autumn rains are a grim time."

"But I don't..." said Romeo. "I've got lots of..."

"I'm not saying I didn't enjoy your company," Selma explained. "But all that is finished now. Goodbye, Sir Romeo."

She turned her back on the poor romantic drone and walked away. Romeo tried to catch up but Selma's guards and fanners and escorts closed in around her and pushed him away. Still Romeo kept struggling to get close to Selma until a few of the escorts buzzed at him in a way that said, "Do you want to see our stings, mister?" Romeo staggered away, moaning.

"Don't cry," Nancy Clancy called to him. "Here. Come up here. We're reading."

All his dreams of knighthood gone, Romeo could hardly climb, but at last he reached us. Though he was a drone bee and Mr Horne was human, he reminded me of Mr Horne staggering along handcuffed.

"I am reading *The Grasshopper's Feast*," Miss Nancy Clancy told him grandly. "Want to listen?"

He slumped down beside Basil. By the time Nancy stopped reading, all the drones were asleep.

18

The Drones are Expelled

"No, I can't do it," Apis told us. "There's no way in which I can feed Basil and Romeo and all those others."

"Why ever not?" asked Miss Nancy Clancy.

"You shouldn't have to ask that. It's because. Because," groaned Apis. "Look, it's like this. One day on the radio at Mrs Abey's place or Mrs Maguire's, I heard that a man had found a lump of amber, and in the amber was the body of a worker bee, and the bee and the amber were forty-three million years old. Now *that* bee never fed drones once the autumn came. For forty-three million years there's never been a worker bee who fed a drone once the rains came down or the snow began. And you want me to start. To take the precious honey that we'll need all winter and give it to drones who never did anything to earn it. I like Romeo. I even like Basil, but liking has nothing to do with it."

I saw that Apis was making the same sort of speech that

Sergeant Kennedy had weeks ago, "I like Jimmy Horne, I even like Clarence Abey. But liking has nothing to do with it."

But I didn't tell her she reminded me of Sergeant Kennedy.

"Besides," she said, "when I fly in with nectar I have to give it over to the hive workers, so that they can run round with it drying it and turning it to honey. You can't ask me to behave like a human, because I'm not. I've got two stomachs. Did you even know that? I have a stomach for myself and a second one for carrying nectar for the hive. The second one doesn't belong to me, it belongs to the hive, and the nectar I carry in it, and the honey I make in it, that all belongs to the hive. Tell me this, can a bank manager, the manager of the National Bank in Northtown say, can he take money out of the bank's safe and go down to the corner of Smith Street and hand it out to anyone he likes?"

"I wish he could," I said, thinking of the Hornes, thinking of my parents too, who were always worrying about money.

"But can he?" said Apis.

"No," I admitted.

"And you would put him in jail if he did. Wouldn't you? You wonderful humans? You'd put him behind bars?"

"I…yes. He'd go to jail."

"There!" said Apis.

Just the same, that afternoon Apis climbed in amongst the drones. "Get in a circle," she told them, "so no one else can see." When they had, she began feeding each of them a small drop of honey from her honey stomach. Some of the drones pushed and struggled to be fed first and Apis roared at them.

"So kind, so kind," said Romeo, taking his honey.

"It's not kind," Apis snarled. "It's stupid. It isn't enough to keep

you strong, I can't *get* enough to keep you strong. So I'm only dragging out the pain."

"Just the same," said Basil, "just the same, thank you."

Poor Basil had changed. He didn't make speeches any more. He was weak but he had what people call dignity.

As Apis left, I asked her. "Why do *we* still get fed?"

"It's different," she said. "You aren't drones."

The next day Nancy Clancy and I offered some of our breakfast to the drones, but they were already too weak to eat. They staggered down to the doorway of the hive as if they needed air and sat there panting. Nancy Clancy and I watched them, angry with ourselves for not being able to help. As the rain boomed down, workers crept up on the drones. Six workers grabbed Basil and began to drag him out of doors. He struggled to stay, his feet clicking against the hard stone of the doorway as the small, well-fed workers hauled him away. They got him over the edge of the door, but he still hung on, staring in at the hive, the home where he wanted to stay all winter. "Selma," he yelled. "Selma!" But Selma didn't answer. With three tough workers grabbing his belly he slid off the rim of the doorway. The other drones lay about, flat on their stomachs, knowing their turn was next, not being able to do anything.

At last the workers threw poor Romeo out. As his body began to slide out the door, he too called to Selma.

"I forgot to ask you, Your Majesty," he yelled. "Who's the oldest settler in the west?"

No one took any notice of him. I heard him squeak out the answer as he fell. "The sun," he called.

When I saw him go, I looked down at the whole hive. I saw that many of the bees had not even noticed that the few drones were now gone. “I hate you!” I screamed. “I hate you, Selma. I hate all of you.”

But no one answered me, except Nancy Clancy.

“It always happens,” she said. “It happens every year. It’s the way things are done.”

She sadly packed her books away and began to yawn. “Why are you yawning?” I asked her savagely. “They just threw your friend Romeo out to starve, and you’re yawning!”

“I always yawn when the autumn rains start. It’s something I can’t help.” While I stood there trembling, Apis appeared in the doorway.

“I want to go home,” I said.

“I’ve come to take you home,” said Apis calmly. “Because it’s time for you to go. The rain has stopped for the moment, so it had better be now.”

“Oh,” I said. I’d thought she would argue, that Nancy Clancy would argue. So it really was the end. They couldn’t afford honey for me either any more.

“I’ll take you back to where I got you from,” said Apis. “Remember, the great white beds and that funny hospital smell?”

“You come too!” I told Nancy Clancy.

Nancy Clancy shook her head sharply. “I thought I’d made it perfectly clear that I can’t do that. What would your parents do with a hundred and twenty year old child? What class would they put me in? No, Apis will find a dry place for me to sleep the winter away, and in the spring—I’ll be collected again.”

“But, will I ever see you?” I asked in a sudden panic. “Will I see you, Apis? Or you Nancy Clancy?”

Apis looked away, which is hard for a bee to do, on account of its large eyes.

"Well," Miss Nancy Clancy admitted, "perhaps you won't, Ned. But we...we have all these happy memories."

"But I want you both to..." I began.

"Get on my back, Ned," said Apis in a final sort of way.

I climbed on to the place where the hair was thickest, just where the chest and stomach meet. Nancy Clancy climbed on behind me, her gingham dress rustling as always.

"I'm just going for the ride," she explained, tears in her eyes.

Apis took off without any delay, without even asking Nancy Clancy not to pull her hair. I didn't say goodbye to Selma, but I didn't want to. And suddenly it was too late. We were out in the dark, out amongst the dripping trees. "Wait!" I called. "Wait! Romeo and Basil must still be here, somewhere."

Apis flapped up and down in the one place so that she could argue with me. "You don't want to see them again," she told me.

"Please find them."

With a grunt of disapproval, Apis began flying low over the wet entangled grass and I called their names. I called Romeo. I called Basil.

We found them close to each other, almost on their sides on the sopping ground. Apis flew in circles around them. I called to them. "Romeo, Basil, I'm going home. I can feed you honey every morning on a silver spoon. Please, get up, get up and follow."

They began to shake themselves. "I promise," I told them.

And so, as Apis and Nancy Clancy and I flew uphill and into the town, Romeo and Basil, using the last of their strength, flapped upwards into the moist air and followed us. Ahead I saw the lights of the hospital go on, and all at once it was hard to see Romeo and Basil as they struggled on behind us. I called to them, but the darkness behind me got deeper. Yet whenever I looked at the hospital, its lights hurt my eyes. "Romeo, Basil!" I kept calling.

Not only did no answer come, but without warning Apis seemed to disappear from beneath me, and I fell spinning between the bright lights of the hospital and the deep wet night.

19

Home

You won't be surprised when I say that I opened my eyes and found that I lay in the hospital bed from which Apis had taken me at the beginning of the summer. Suddenly waking up in bed is something that happens in all stories like mine, and the only difference is that my story happened, whereas the others were dreamed up.

The fierce Sister was looking at me through eyes that were nearly closed. She was counting and holding my wrist. The screens were still in place around my bed, as they had been all that time ago.

"Lie still, Ned," said the Sister. "Doctor Morgan's going to be very happy. He's been worried about you."

She went, in fact almost rushed, out through the screens. In half a minute she was back with Doctor Morgan and my mother and father. Seeing them, I knew I was back amongst my kind and a warmth as golden as any honey ran through my body.

"Thank God," my mother said, kissing me.

"You had us very worried," my father told me, while the doctor himself felt pulses in my head and asked if this or that hurt.

"You were in what they call a coma, darling," my mother told me. "That's a long sleep. You slept for weeks. But you're awake now."

"Have you seen a girl in a gingham dress?" I asked them, starting to cry, because I'd just understood that although I was back with my people, I'd seen Nancy Clancy and Apis for the last time ever.

"No, no," said my father. He asked the Sister. "Did you see a girl?"

They tried to tell me about how sick I'd been, and how a doctor had been brought from Port Macquarie to look at me. And every time I tried to say something about Selma or Romeo or the hive they butted in and told me more about my illness and what the Port Macquarie doctor had said and how I had nothing to fear—that I'd be a normal child again. I wondered what a normal child was. Was Maurie Abey a normal child? In any case, the normal child I wanted to see was Nancy Clancy. And she was a hundred and twenty years old.

It was when I asked them about Mr Horne that they stopped talking.

"Did they put Mr Horne in jail?" I asked suddenly.

There was silence. They had at last forgotten about the doctor from Port Macquarie.

"For stealing Morrison's prize bull?" I explained.

"How did you know about that?" my father asked. "How did

he know about that?" he asked the doctor.

Doctor Morgan explained. "He must have overheard you talking about it here one day when you were visiting. There are different levels of coma. He must have been not quite fully unconscious for a few seconds and heard about Mr Horne that way."

I said, "But I saw it. I saw it from a hole in the wall at Major Steel's old house. There was Jimmy Horne, Clarence Abey and the bull Fred. Then Morrison and Sergeant Kennedy came and arrested them."

I saw the adults looking at each other in their strange adult way.

"I sent you a letter," I told them.

I saw that look on their faces again.

"A letter?" said my father.

"I left it at Miss Such's place for her to give you."

"Oh," my mother said, "Miss Such has left here. She's gone to England on a liner."

"But they all helped me write it. Nancy and Apis and Romeo and Basil's boys..."

My father shook his head. "We didn't get any letter, cobber."

He was the first one to decide not to waste his time wondering. "Anyhow," he said, "Morrison decided he'd let Jimmy Horne off if Jimmy and Abey worked for him free one day a week for the next five years. It's a hard bargain, but it's better than being in jail."

Soon I went to Sydney and doctors examined my head, finding nothing very wrong with it. But the life I'd lived in the hive stays with me still. Every spring I wonder if Nancy Clancy is waking and if a bee like Apis is collecting her to take her to a hive for another bee summer. Every autumn I leave out honey for drones that are thrown out of their hives but they don't seem to eat much of it. Perhaps Apis was right, and you can't do much about things that have been happening for forty-three million years. Whenever I see a bee working on a flower, I think of Apis, who probably did not live through that winter, for worker bees have short, hard but, I think, happy lives.

As you can see I've never forgotten Apis or Romeo, Basil or Selma, and that's why I've written this book. And as for Nancy Clancy: "Oh Miss Clancy, I know you're alive, and rhyming still in some summer hive."

NOTE ABOUT THE AUTHOR

AUSTRALIAN BORN author Thomas Keneally has published over 25 novels, which have spanned five continents and covered topics ranging from the Armistice talks following World War I to a young woman's flight to the Australian Outback .

Schindler's List is probably Keneally's best know work of fiction, a moving account of Oscar Schindler's attempt to rescue Jews during World War II for which he was awarded the Booker Prize for Fiction in 1982 and the Los Angeles Times Prize for Fiction in 1983.

Keneally has also composed travel narratives, written more than a dozen screenplays, and had his work has been translated into every published language. This is his only children's book.

Ned Kelly & the City of the Bees
has been set in Minion,
a contemporary digital type family
created by Adobe designer
Robert Slimbach.
Minion is inspired by classic old style typefaces
of the late Renaissance
named after one of the type sizes used
in the early days of typefounding.
Minion means "a beloved servant,"
reflecting the type's useful
and unobtrusive qualities.